Gnat Stokes
and the
Foggy Bottom
Swamp Queen

Gnat Stokes

and the
FOGGY BOTTOM
SWAMP QUEEN

Sally M. Keehn

Philomel Books

Sally M. Keehn

PATRICIA LEE GAUCH, EDITOR

PHILOMEL BOOKS
A division of Penguin Young Readers Group. Published by The Penguin Group.
Penguin Group (USA) Inc., 375 Hudson Street, New York, NY 10014, U.S.A.
Penguin Group (Canada), 10 Alcorn Avenue, Toronto, Ontario, Canada M4V 3B2
    (a division of Pearson Penguin Canada Inc.)
Penguin Books Ltd, 80 Strand, London WC2R 0RL, England.
Penguin Ireland, 25 St. Stephen's Green, Dublin 2, Ireland (a division of Penguin
    Books Ltd.)
Penguin Books India Pvt Ltd, 11 Community Centre, Panchsheel Park, New
    Delhi - 110 017, India.
Penguin Group (NZ), Cnr Airborne and Rosedale Roads, Albany, Auckland, New
    Zealand (a division of Pearson New Zealand Ltd).
Penguin Books (South Africa) (Pty) Ltd, 24 Sturdee Avenue, Rosebank, Johannes-
    burg 2196, South Africa.
Penguin Books Ltd, Registered Offices: 80 Strand, London WC2R 0RL, England.

Published simultaneously in Canada. Printed in the United States of America.
Design by Semadar Megged.   The text is set in 12-point Aldus Roman.
Library of Congress Cataloging-in-Publication Data
Keehn, Sally M.
Gnat Stokes and the Foggy Bottom Swamp Queen / Sally M. Keehn.   p. cm.
Summary: In Mary's Cove, Tennessee, in 1869, twelve-year-old Gnat Stokes decides
to prove she's not just a troublemaker by rescuing a boy who was spirited away
seven years earlier by the evil Swamp Queen of Foggy Bottom.
[1. Adventure and adventurers—Fiction. 2. Magic—Fiction. 3. Swamps—Fiction.
4. Cats—Fiction. 5. Tennessee—History—19th century—Fiction.] I. Title.
PZ7.K2257Gna 2005   [Fic]—dc22   2003026635   ISBN 0-399-24287-2
10 9 8 7 6 5 4 3

FOR MY DAUGHTER ALISON—
A KINDRED SPIRIT

1

It's been almost seven years since Zelda, dark queen of them Foggy Bottom Swampers, stole away our peaceful-natured Goodlow Pryce. According to Granny Hart, who collects our stories here in Mary's Cove, our Goodlow was taken on October 31, 1861, barely six months after the War between the States began. On that October day, twelve-year-old Goodlow was out back of his cabin, making raft-boats out of kindling for baby crayfish so's they could go on exploration journeys down Tucker Creek. Goodlow always liked making playthings for little creatures, Granny says.

She says being the thoughtful sort, Goodlow no doubt decided to follow Tucker Creek to see what his crayfish might come upon in their journey. He moseyed past Hallelujah Pond, crossed over Tucker Creek at Piney Gap Ford and then headed down old Piney Gap Road itself, which meanders along the creek. We all know that road can be real dangerous, seeing as how it also skirts the murky edge of Foggy Bottom—that low-lying marshland where Goodlow knew he was not allowed on account of that evil Zelda and them strange folk of hers, them Swampers, who'd slunk in several years earlier and claimed the place for their own.

How do we know Goodlow headed into Foggy Bottom itself, where the mud's as black as a catfish and the fog so thick, the sun don't never burn it off? Well we know because after Goodlow had gone missing, his pappy, Luther, followed Goodlow's footprints and that's where they led and stopped! No one could mistake them footprints, the way Goodlow toed-out. I was only five years old that time he disappeared and now I'm twelve and running amok, but still, even I remember Goodlow's walking style.

His footprints ended at a wild bee tree, which rises from the Foggy Bottom muck like a granny woman reaching out to catch a baby! And them footprints was never seen again. Not until this very afternoon. And only by me and my friends the three Darnell young 'uns. But I'm getting ahead of myself, which I'm inclined to do when I get fired up and surely I am fired up now. I mean to save Goodlow from that evil Swamp Queen and bring him home, thereby making amends for who I am and a terrible wrong I done a week ago last Tuesday. Instead of folks whispering among themselves, "That Gnat Stokes! She's nothing but a no-good misbegotten child, born to raise trouble," they'll be saying, "Gnat Stokes? She's our hero." Wish I could be that hero right now, but I know I got a journey ahead of me filled with pitfalls and great danger.

2

Now, Granny Hart says folks could tell right off it was Zelda who'd stole away our Goodlow because that show-off of a Swamp Queen couldn't keep it to herself. She'd clawed her initial—a large ragged-looking Z—in the wild bee tree right above the spot where Goodlow's footsteps had disappeared! Beneath that Z, Zelda had clawed two words which struck terror in everyone's hearts:

Goodlow's mine.

Soon as he saw them words, Goodlow's pappy got together what few men the war had left in Mary's Cove and they formed a posse to get Goodlow back. With our Chief Constable DeWitt Lawson in the lead and carrying a cross he said would protect them all from the heathen Zelda and her Swampers, they combed Foggy Bottom and nearby Old Baldy Top, that mighty mountain riddled with caves that the wild swamp skirts. Not finding Goodlow in any of these places, the posse trudged up and down all the misty ridges that surround our little cove—tucked up so high here in these Tennessee mountains, you'd think it was a cloud. But they never found our Goodlow nowhere.

DeWitt Lawson said no doubt the Swamp Queen had cast a spell and turned Goodlow into something real peculiar—probably a Swamp Knight. Zelda's fond of them Swamp Knights. She's got an army of them. As a Swamp Knight, Goodlow's fair skin would now be warty and blotched gray-green like a tree frog's, his large dark eyes would be popped out just like a dusky salamander's and he'd creak whenever he moved or clashed swords with them other knights because of the rusted armor he now wore. We'd never see the peaceful-natured Goodlow we knew EVER AGAIN!

When Goodlow's momma heard this, I'm told she died from sorrow on the spot. After giving her as decent a burial as they could without a preacher (them no-good Rebels had done run off our Preacher John for being a Union man), the people of Mary's Cove fenced off Piney Gap Road where it fords Tucker Creek so as not to lose another precious soul to Zelda. DeWitt Lawson painted a sign—Keep Out! This Means You! And Goodlow's pappy, Luther, took to painting polka dots.

You can see Luther's polka-dotted cabin from just about every home in Mary's Cove—sitting as his cabin does up on a little ridge with Old Baldy Top lurking high above. Luther has painted polka dots on most everything inside and outside his two-room cabin—

even and including Goodlow's oak tree with its rope swing from which Goodlow and his sweetheart, Penelope Drinkwater, would hurl themselves into Tucker Creek—the water there being cool and deep.

A while back, I asked Luther why he'd taken to painting polka dots on everything and he said to me, "Gnat, my gal, one day them polka dots is going to draw my Goodlow home."

"What makes you say that?" I asked.

"Them Swamp Knights love polka dots," he said, and I took his word for gospel. Luther owns up to the truth and tells it exactly as he sees it. Always has. Unlike DeWitt Lawson—our chief constable and justice of the peace. That DeWitt Lawson would sooner condemn a gal like me to the Francis Spittle Home for Wayward Girls in Hell on Earth, Tennessee, than own up to the fact that I'm human and I can make mistakes. Same as him. Same as everybody.

3

I don't think it was Luther's polka dots that drew our Goodlow back to Mary's Cove this very afternoon—October 28, 1868—with maple leaves tipped red like fire. Nope. It was Penelope Drinkwater's lovelorn sighs and I'll tell you why I think I know, but you can't tell no one, you hear?

THIS MUST BE KEPT SECRET!

Now I'd been out gathering walnuts along with my friends the three Darnell young 'uns—Wanda, Jib (who is a gal) and Baby Earl, eleven, nine and three, respectively. Whenever they ain't working for their momma, them Darnells can be found with me. They eat supper and sleep with me at night—have ever since their brother Studs returned home from the war, testy as a cross-eyed snake. He threw them young 'uns out of their bed so's he could have it for his own! He made them sleep on the cold hard floor! When I saw this, I said, "Wanda, Jib and Baby Earl, why don't you come on and stay with my Grandpa Stokes and me?"

So they did.

Now, them Darnells and me—we'd just about filled our baskets with walnuts when all of a sudden-like we came upon some queer-looking footprints in the mud along our side of Tucker Creek—Foggy Bottom looming forth, dark and silent, from the other. It didn't take me a minute to figure out they were Goodlow's footprints, all toed-out the way they were. I got real excited! But Jib was fit to be tied! Jib shrieked, "Them footprints belong to Zelda's Boogety Bear! Run! Guard your backsides! Cover your innards!"

The *Boogety Bear* is Jib's name for Zelda's Foggy Bottom Swamp Guard who looks like a bear and his heart beats so loud, you'd think it was the heartbeat of the marshland—*boogety, boogety.* I ain't never seen this bear myself, but I've heard him! The sound he makes as he prowls unseen through the Foggy Bottom mist is enough to chill my bone marrow.

Course, I knew them footprints didn't belong to no Boogety Bear. So I grabbed Jib's arm, threw her to the ground and sat on her to settle her down a bit. I studied the footprints in order to gather surefire evidence, and I found it. I pointed out to all three Darnells that a bear, even a Boogety Bear that's been seen to walk upright on his two hind legs like a man and he's got long gray fur that gleams through the dark like fox fire, would leave claw marks, which these footprints didn't have.

With Jib clinging to my one arm, Wanda clinging to

the other and Baby Earl holding on to my apron strings, we slunk down low and tiptoed after them footprints because we didn't want Zelda nor any Swamper hidden in the Foggy Bottom mist to sense what we were up to. This wasn't as easy as it might sound because all three Darnells kept tripping on me.

We tracked them footprints to the hollowed-out log in Tucker Creek where Penelope Drinkwater spends time washing clothes, combing out her long yellow hair and pining away the afternoons with sighing after Goodlow. She's been sighing after him for almost seven years. As I said earlier, them two were sweethearts.

Penelope's sighs must have finally broken through whatever spell Zelda had cast over that poor stolen boy, because, on Penelope's hollowed-out washing log, he'd spelled out in red and white streaked beans that he must have somehow stole from my Grandpa Stokes's bean shed, because only my grandpa grows beans like these— PENELOPE. U R MY TRUE LUV. SAVE ME FROM ZELDA. MEET ME HERE. 2 NIGHT. MIDNITE.

I read this message that I just happened to find before Penelope did two times—once in silence to myself; once out loud for them Darnells because they don't know how to read. And it came to me during the second reading that I, Gnat Stokes, should be the one to save Goodlow from the Swamp Queen—not Penelope. This might surprise you seeing as how that gal is Goodlow's true love and Granny Hart, who has the second sight (which means she sees things others can't), has told me often enough, "One day true love will defeat the Swamp Queen and bring our Goodlow back.

"Gnat, believe in love."

Having had my share of heartache, I ain't altogether sure I can believe in love, true or otherwise. Besides which, Goodlow's true love is too easy natured to fight off any Swamp Queen. That Penelope don't have a fighting bone in her. And she's shortsighted, too. She can't see but two feet in front of her—them two feet being her own!

Nope. I'd meet Goodlow at the washing log myself. I'd save him from Zelda myself. I'm scrappy. I like a good fight and I see better than most. By saving Goodlow, I'd redeem myself for all the wrongs I ever did. So I pocketed the beans and swore the three Darnells to secrecy—"Don't you tell Penelope about this message nor anyone at Mary's Cove neither or else I won't let you spend the night with me ever again nor read to you from *Ten Nights in a Bar-Room and I Was There*!"

Them Darnells love for me to read to them, so they don't say nothing to nobody. Nope. Not for the entire day and into the night.

4

It's drawing onto midnight and here we are—the four of us—me, Wanda, Jib and Baby Earl—sneaking out the back door of Grandpa Stokes's cabin. This ain't what I had planned. I'd planned on meeting Goodlow by myself. But just as soon as them Darnells got their reading to— that being the last part of the first chapter of *Ten Nights in a Bar-Room* in which the dangers of drinking are made known and you'd best stay away from a tavern named *The Sickle and Sheaf*—Wanda cleared her throat and she said, "Gnat? Who's saving Goodlow Pryce tonight?"

In a truthful mood, I said, "I am."

And that Wanda, always loyal to me, said, "Then me, Jib and Baby Earl are coming along with you as body-guards."

I said, "I don't need no bodyguards."

And that Wanda said, "Yes you do."

Jib, licking her skinny lips, said, "If you don't take us with you, we'll wake up your grandpa and tell him what you're up to. He'll tan your hide good! You know you ain't supposed to be out gallivanting after dark! Not after what you done a week ago last Tuesday."

I couldn't have no one waking up my grandpa! So here I am with my three bodyguards even though I carry surefire protection from Zelda in my apron pocket—two iron nails wrought together to form a cross and, just in case that don't work, a pint of Grandpa's moonshine whiskey to throw into her eyes and melt them.

A three-quarter moon shines, making shadows out of everything, including Grandpa's cow Ida Blue. Her bell rings forlornly through the cool night air. Fallen leaves crackle underfoot and there's just enough wind to make you shiver as it slips through the trees—*beware, beware* . . .

"Gnat, I'm scairt," Wanda whispers in my ear.

"When Zelda finds out what we're up to, she'll eat out our eyeballs," Jib says.

"Yup, and she'll tear apart our innards same way she did Uncle Hershorn's cow," Wanda says.

"Then she'll set her Boogety Bear upon us. He'll gnaw the meat off all our bones—clavicles and all," Jib says.

Only Baby Earl says nothing because even though he's three, he don't ever talk.

I stop at Grandpa's bean shed, and I turn to the three Darnells. "I didn't ask you to come with me." I finger the iron cross and flask inside my apron pocket. "Just go on back to the cabin, climb up to the loft and wait for me there."

"But you're our best friend," Wanda says.

"Friends stick together," Jib says, and that Baby Earl takes me by the hand and looks up at me so sweet, it's like to break my heart.

"All right, then. Come and go with me. But no more talk about being scairt." We stack our hands, one on top of the other—"One potato, two potato, three potato, four." Then us four friends head bravely out through the eerie moonlit night toward Tucker Creek and Penelope's washing log.

Soon, I, Gnat Stokes, will save Goodlow Pryce from the wicked Zelda.

Soon I'll be a hero.

5

ary's Cove, surrounded as it is by high blue-misted mountain ridges, ain't that big. Only sixty-three homesteads, an empty church with its nearby Hallelujah Pond (once used for holy baptisms) and a burnt-down schoolhouse strung out along a nine-mile loop road with Tucker Creek along the south side of the loop. Before war tore our cove apart with thirteen of our able-bodied menfolk, including my own no-good pappy, joining them thieving Rebels, we had eighty-three homesteads with a full church and a little red schoolhouse where students would recite their ABCs. (Wish we still had that schoolhouse. I'd like a school with a teacher who'd keep my gnat-brain occupied.)

And we had the prettiest rainbow, which would appear after every rainstorm. We ain't seen that rainbow now for almost seven years. It disappeared the day Zelda stole away our Goodlow. You see, Goodlow and Penelope together formed the pot of gold at the rainbow's end. That's how the story goes. And once that pot of gold was gone, the rainbow didn't have no place to land.

We all miss that rainbow. Still, even without it, our spit of land is satisfying to the eye. It's almost flat with meadows of clover grass, fields of corn, apple trees and fenced-in garden patches rolling gently down to Tucker Creek. On the far side of that creek and just across Piney Gap Road stands Foggy Bottom. You could lose yourself in that strange dark bottomland with its twisted trees, strangler vines, thick brush, endless mud and deep pools of standing water. Unlike most mountain swamps that ain't all that big, Foggy Bottom stretches for miles and miles. It skirts Old Baldy Top Mountain with its caverns and then plunges down, down across the state line to Gobbler's Glen, North Carolina—a place where my pappy once worked a copper mine.

I was born in Foggy Bottom.

My momma, whoever she is, placed me in a basket on the front porch of my pappy's boardinghouse in Gobbler's Glen with a note: *Hiram Stokes, this child, born in Foggy Bottom, is yours.* I've often wondered who my momma is and does she ever wonder about me? Once I become a hero, maybe she'll catch wind of it and finally come to visit. Only now, as I close in on Tucker Creek, I'm finding it real hard to think like a hero because Wanda has the sneezes. No matter how many times I hiss, "Wanda, you got to stop them sneezes," they keep right on coming even though she's stuck two fingers up her nose.

As for Jib? She's wearing a pair of hand-me-down shoes. Them shoes is just too big for her and she can't walk right in them. They make shuffle noises and she won't take them off and go barefoot like the rest of us because she's suddenly decided she don't like the feel of dirt between her toes.

Worse still, Grandpa Stokes fed Baby Earl too many beans at supper. "You got to eat more beans," my grandpa told that little boy. Grandpa kept on and on, "Eat more beans." So now the farts have come on Baby Earl and I can't hiss at him to stop because he'll cry.

I can't be a hero with these Darnells! These Darnells make too much noise! At the oak tree with three bullets in its trunk from where that Rebel Frank Gump and his Stuart Hollow Boys tried to ambush my Grandpa Stokes four years ago and failed, I stop and I tell the Darnells, "You've come far enough. Your job now is to wait here. I'll go on down to Penelope's washing log, save Goodlow and be back with him in two shakes of a lamb's tail. Do not follow me, you understand?" I fix them Darnells with what Grandpa calls my General Ulysses S. Grant stare—firm and solid, but with just a lick of danger in it.

Them Darnells say nothing. That nothing speaks louder than a fart or sneeze.

"You can't come along with me!" I hiss at them. "You can't! You'll awaken Zelda's Warrior Bogies!"

Baby Earl's lower lip starts to quiver and so I don't go on to describe them bogies. My grandpa's friend Buffer McLeod (he runs a secret moonshine operation along the murky edge of Foggy Bottom, but don't tell no one or you'll get him in trouble) has seen them Warrior Bogies up close. Buffer says they look like rotted tree stumps to trip you up only they got catfish heads and a large tentacle that can sting you blind.

"And if them Warrior Bogies don't get you," I say, "the Boogety Bear will! So wait right here, I'll bring you Goodlow." I walk away before them Darnells can try and stop me. The wind picks up. The wind blows hard into my face—*go back, go back* . . .

I go on. Without them Darnells tagging along, I make my way through a tangle of dog-hobble and downhill toward Tucker Creek with such stealth, you'd think I was a stalking panther, which is what Zelda can turn herself into if she has a mind to. Her panther claws can rake your backside to the bone, so you'd best not try to turn from her and flee.

I ain't scairt of Zelda. I ain't scairt of nothing. This past July, I faced a Rebel bushwhacker with hunger in his eyes, a half-moon scar on his right cheek and he was holding a fifteen-gauge shotgun pointed at me. And do you know who that Rebel was? My own pappy! That dirty bushwhacker! I screamed at him, "You get away!

There ain't no place in Mary's Cove for the likes of you! In Mary's Cove, it's the Union forever!"

"I accept that, Gnat," he said. I didn't believe him. I never will. He's a no-good Rebel and he always will be. He said, "I was just hoping to pay you and my own pappy a visit. After all, the war's been over for three years and I'm real sorry it happened.

"I brought something special for you." My pappy reached into his ragged shirt and brought out an ugly old sow's ear tied up with a horse tail hair like it was a present! He tried to hand it to me! He said, "It came in your baby basket. It's your momma's gift to you— meant for you now you've turned twelve. You got to take it, Gnat," he said.

"Why do I got to?" I said.

"Because it's meant for you," he said.

"First, tell me who my momma is," I said and he said, like always, "You know I don't know. I'd had but one night with her and I'd been drinking. But I'll tell you this. I loved that woman harder than I've loved any and I ain't loved another since. I'd give my eyeteeth to see her once again. She had wild red hair like yours and she loved my fiddle playing."

"Well, I'll tell you something!" I said. "My momma would never leave me something wrapped up in an old sow's ear! She wouldn't!" Then I shouted for Grandpa— out plowing the back field. Grandpa, a Union man, and

Pappy, a no-good Rebel, get along like oil on fire especially when I ain't willing to put myself between them.

Grandpa came running and my pappy turned and fled. Later, I hid myself in a pile of hay and cried. Used to be, before the war, my pappy would visit me and Grandpa every few months from that North Carolina copper mine he worked. He'd swing me high above his head—*How's my little Gnat?* He brought me clackers! I'd keep time with them clackers while he played his fiddle! We had some fun!

Then he took up with them Stuart Hollow Boys— Rebels all. Them fools had deserted the Union because, they said, it took away their freedom. They planned on making Gobbler's Glen, North Carolina, the capital of the Confederate States of America, and they were willing to take on all Union-minded folk to do it! They ambushed Mary's Cove because most of our folk are and always will be loyal to the Union, they ran our preacher out of town, and they burned down our schoolhouse. . . .

6

The wind blows off Foggy Bottom—smelling like a wet dog's fur. Tree branches clatter overhead—*go back*. I go bravely onward toward Tucker Creek. Ahead of me, moonlit fingers of Foggy Bottom mist reach across the gurgling creek like they want to grab me up and carry me off somewheres. The damp wind moving through the trees repeats their warning: *Go back. Go back.*

Ain't no warning gonna stop me. I draw close to Penelope's washing log, but I don't see Goodlow nowhere. The wind, growing stronger still, fills with the buzz of angry swamp voices. I've been warned that them Swampers, even Zelda's tiny polka-dotted Swamp Faeries who ride the backs of stinkpot turtles, are strong enough to pluck you up and carry you away. Fear prickles my skin and makes my heart pound as I bring out my cross of nails. I hold it up into the wind and I cry out to protect myself, "God Bless You All!

"God bless you and bring me Goodlow Pryce!"

There's a horrible screech—like a panther at rutting time—and something comes hurtling toward me through the damp night air. Being the true hero that I am, I bravely hold out my hands and I catch that something. It's not what I expect—a real-life boy. It feels soft and plump and furry and it's smaller than a baby lamb. It's got a rounded head with funny-looking ears that turn down at the tips and a locket dangling from a necklace it's got clenched between its teeth.

Wanda, all out of breath from running over to me, pants into my face, "Gnat! That don't look like Goodlow Pryce."

Jib, carrying Baby Earl, joins us, saying, "Gnat, I think you done caught yourself a cat." She leans in for a closer look, draws in her breath and then she shrieks at me, "That cat's got poison juices dripping from its fangs! That cat will bite and kill you! Throw it to the snapping turtles!"

7

Well, I ain't about to feed a poor cat, now scairt to death by Jib, to a nasty snapping turtle. At least not yet. The cat's trembling. It's trying to hide its rounded head underneath my right arm. After some consideration of it, I say, "Jib, them ain't poison juices dripping from its fangs. Them's just drool mixed with a necklace that's got a golden locket stuck to it."

"It ain't natural for a cat to have a necklace with a golden locket." Wanda closes her left eye, bulges out her right and eyeballs the cat. Baby Earl, still in Jib's arms, eyeballs the cat, too. The cat burrows so tight against me, I expect to feel the beating of its scairt little heart against my big brave one, but I don't feel any heartbeat at all. This strikes me as real peculiar.

Wanda grabs hold of the locket and tries to pull it away from the cat. It holds on the determined way a dog with a bone would and so Wanda lifts the locket up into the moonlight with the cat's mouth still attached. It's a pretty heart-shaped locket with one word writ on the

front. I read that word out loud for them Darnells—
"*Penelope.* The locket says *Penelope.*"

"Oh no!" Wanda exclaims. "Oh no! Oh no!"

"What is it, Wanda?" I say.

"I think Goodlow was bringing the locket to give to
Penelope, them Swampers caught him up and then . . .
and then you shouted, 'God bless you,' which got them
Swampers mad, so they worked a spell on Goodlow and
changed him to a cat."

"Do you know this for a fact?" I say. Wanda is always
one for making up facts.

She says, "I do," and them other two nod.

"Well, I ain't worried." This is a lie. Course I'm worried. I went out to save a boy and got him changed into
a cat. But I ain't the kind to admit defeat. As I carry the
cat with his dangling necklace away from the now silent
Foggy Bottom mist and back to my grandpa's cabin with
them Darnells making all their customary noises alongside me, I ponder the situation. Maybe, in the soft and
comforting light of my kerosene lantern, I can work a
spell to change Goodlow back to his rightful nature. I
ain't never worked a spell, but, as I explain to them Darnells, "You just never know what you are capable of
until you give it a try."

8

It's a good thing Grandpa Stokes and his dog Ida Red are hard of hearing. Otherwise they'd take notice of me and them Darnells sneaking through the cabin's back door and making our noisy way up the stairs by the chimney to my sleeping loft and there'd be hell to pay!

I set the cat down on my corn shuck mattress that's big enough for them Darnells to share with me at night and under which I hide two books I read aloud at bedtime: *Ten Nights in a Bar-Room*, which I mentioned earlier and which I swiped from DeWitt Lawson's parlor. And *Robert Burns's Complete Poetical Works*, which I borrowed from Buffer McLeod only he don't know it and I ain't proud of that. It's just that I'm real fond of books and I can't seem to keep my hands off them. Wish I could understand all what these books have to offer me. I need me a teacher to help me out. I want to understand this world I'm in and learn to do what's right.

Wanda lights my lantern and in its revealing glow I can now see Goodlow real clear-like. Goodlow's a gray tabby cat with small turned-down ears and dark-furred rings along his body and tail. He seems right at home on my bed. He kneads the quilt Granny Hart handed me on my twelfth birthday. The quilt's made up of colorful squares sewn by the women of Mary's Cove. Granny had each one sew her name on the square she made. Granny said, "This gift's given to you from all us women in Mary's Cove. You are our Gnat and don't you forget it."

How can I forget I'm their Gnat when I got names like Vera May Clauser, Sophie Drinkwater, Lila Sparks and Granny Hart sleeping on top of me? The thought of all them women watching over me is enough to give me headaches. The cat, necklace still dangling from his mouth, proceeds to sit himself down upon the one quilt square that should have a name stitched on it, but it don't—my momma's. I like to think her name is *Jenny Lind*. I once saw Jenny Lind's likeness in a Barnum and Bailey circus poster and I thought, She looks like a momma should—real pretty and with a soft sweet smile. Jenny Lind's a famous singer. Famous singers move from one concert hall to the next, so they don't have time for raising young 'uns.

The cat's regarding me with big gold eyes.

"What spell you gonna use to change the cat into a real-life boy?" Wanda asks me.

"Well, Wanda," I say. "I've been thinking on this the whole way home. What comes to mind is a changing spell Buffer once heard Zelda say. One moment, the Swamp Queen towered over Buffer's moonshine still with her long red hair hanging free, skin white as the dead and eyes the color of pale green cornmeal. The next, she muttered the spell, went pop like a pig bladder that's just been stuck and turned herself into a panther! Buffer said she said—"

"Wait! Don't say them words!" shouts Jib. "Them words will cause Goodlow here to change into a panther! He'll eat out our eyeballs. He'll suck out our brains through our empty eyeball sockets!"

"Whisper them words to me, Gnat," Wanda says and so I do, " 'Pzzzaaaattt to that—I am now a cat!' "

"Well, that's easy," Wanda says. "We just need to say a backwards spell that will change Goodlow back to what he was before he was a cat." She diddles her skinny fingers over his head and says, "Oh for joy! You are now a boy!"

It don't work. Course it don't work! Wanda didn't do it right! I turn my back on the cat and whisper to Wanda so he don't hear, "I think it's Zelda's spell said *exactly* backwards—*Cat a now am I—that to pzzzaaaattt!* But to make it work right, we need to say it while picturing Goodlow the way he used to be—as a boy."

"We can't remember what he looked like then! It's been too long since we last seen him," Wanda wails.

"We could remember," I say. "If we got hold of that

locket necklace he don't seem to want to let go of no matter what. Lockets keep pictures in them of our dear and/or departed for when we're lonesome and need to take a look at them. I'm almost certain that locket holds a picture of Goodlow like he was before Zelda stole him."

"How you gonna get the locket from him?" Jib says.

"I need to think on that." I stare at the cat. He's got what looks like two dark-furred pitchforks on his forehead, which gives him a real intense expression. He could be a stalwart adversary. Wanda eyeballs him. Jib sits on the floor, takes off her shoes and rubs her sore feet. Baby Earl tugs on my hand. I say, "Baby Earl, what do you want?"

He hands me a tin plate with part of the dessert portion of his supper meal that he couldn't finish—mashed beans with cream. He points to the cat.

"You want that I should feed this here cat your beans and cream?" I ask.

Baby Earl nods.

"Baby Earl, you are not only a generous boy, but a real smart one, too." A cat can't eat with a golden necklace hanging from his mouth. He'll have to drop it first. I turn to the cat and say, "You've had a hard night. You must be powerful hungry." I place the plate of beans and cream in front of him. "Now you go on and eat. You go on and eat them beans and cream!" He drops the necklace with the locket on my quilt—just like that—and starts in to eat.

Before the cat realizes what he's done, I grab up the necklace and put it on over my neck so's he can't take it back. As soon as the heart-shaped locket marked *Penelope* strikes my chest, a queer feeling comes over me—something I've never felt before. Why, this locket must be enchanted. Wearing it makes me want to hug a boy and cover him with kisses!

"Open the locket!" Wanda and Jib both scream and so I do. There ain't no picture of Goodlow inside it. There's only a tiny piece of paper with even tinier writing on it:

Cat nos the way 2 me. I luv u, Goodlow.

9

Everyone's asleep but me. Jib spoons Wanda's back, a snoring Wanda spoons mine, I spoon Baby Earl's and he spoons the cat, curled up so tight against him, it's hard to tell where boy ends and cat begins. How this cat will lead me to Goodlow Pryce I do not know, but I mean to find out and I will.

Goodlow's the boy the golden locket makes me want to hug and kiss. I know that now and glory be, Goodlow ain't a cat! The cat is Goodlow's messenger. I've just woke up from dreaming about that precious boy and I ache to be with him. I've got his name on my lips and his likeness burned into my heart. If this ain't true love, I don't know what is.

Goodlow wrote, I luv u.

Now I ain't never believed in love—though Granny Hart has talked to me about it. Has she talked! Over and over—whenever she holds me captive in her washtub and scrubs the layers of dirt off me. Granny calls love a sparkling crystal with more sides to it than you can count. One side's the love that causes you to put someone else's needs above your own. Granny's sermonized me about this side so much, it's grown tiresome. Another side's the caring love between two friends. Another still's a love for home and family. And then, you got the love between two sweethearts that sets the world on fire.

I feel like I've swallowed the love crystal whole and I got the sweetheart side pressed against my heart. I clutch the golden locket the cat brought to my burning heart. Goodlow made this locket. I'm sure he made it and he poured all his love into it when he did. This locket is love-enchanted. Why else would it cause me to fall in love and dream about this boy I ain't seen since I was five?

Penelope's boy.

If that ain't a conundrum, I don't know what is.

In my dream, Zelda had locked Goodlow up in one of them dark caverns of hers—inside Old Baldy Top. We all know she holds court inside them caverns. We've heard her panther scream coming from in there. We've felt the deep underground rumble of horses' hooves as she and her Swampers gallop up and up and out of the mountain and into Foggy Bottom.

I dreamt I came upon Goodlow lying inside a small cold underground mountain cave, lit only by a single torchlight. He slept on the dirt hard floor, which broke my heart. He wore a bearskin robe and he had a thick leather collar around his neck by which he was chained to a bolt in the wall. This made my broken heart ache so bad, I felt as if it was me, in chains.

I ventured up to Goodlow and he lifted his big dark eyes to look at me. His dark hair swept back from his pale and handsome face in beautiful ringlets. He whispered, *"Cat knows the way to me. Hurry to me. All Hallows' Eve draws near."*

"All Hallows' Eve?" I said to him in my dream. He nodded like I knew exactly what All Hallows' Eve had in store for him and so I acted like I did. I do know that on that fearful night Zelda and her Swampers parade through Mary's Cove on their way to the Devil's Notch on South Mountain where they light bonfires and carry on loud enough to raise the devil himself. I said to Goodlow, "Don't worry. I got three days 'til All Hallows' Eve. Soon as the cat wakes up and shows me how to get to you, I'll be at your side."

Goodlow reached out then and he stroked my cheek. I ain't never had no one stroke my cheek! Not even Granny Hart, who helped Grandpa Stokes in raising me. I thought, Goodlow loves me! I love Goodlow and he loves me back! This got me so excited, it woke me up. I tell you, it's one thing to save a boy from a Swamp Queen because you want to defeat her and be a hero. It's another still to do it because you're in love with the boy. Pile one on top of the other and you have a fiery conflagration of the heart!

I'm so in love with Goodlow, I don't wake up the Darnells to tell them about it. See? I'm already practicing that side of love Granny has drilled into me—putting someone else's needs above my own. Them Darnells do need their sleep. Besides which, if I was to tell them I loved Goodlow, that Wanda would say, "But Gnat, Goodlow ain't your sweetheart," which would make me feel real guilty.

And that Jib, who likes to exaggerate a situation until she comes up with the worst of the worst, would make me feel even guiltier by saying, "Gnat, if you steal Goodlow from Penelope, you'll break her heart. She'll cry so hard, she'll cause a flood. Them floodwaters will wash away our topsoil so's we can't grow our corn and beans. We won't have nothing to eat and all of Mary's Cove will starve."

10

At dawn, after fussing with me because I said, "If the cat takes off for Goodlow while you're gone for the day, I'll have to follow him without you," them three Darnells stomp off to work for their momma. It ain't my fault if they can't go along with me and the cat! It's Ma Darnell's. Ma Darnell's law states them three young 'uns can spend nights with me. They spend their days doing chores for her. With her husband dead from an old war wound, Studs too mean and lazy to help out and a family to care for, Ma Darnell has more chores than you can shake a stick at.

Still, even though I'm love-struck and anxious to go after Goodlow, I do miss them Darnells soon as they leave. I always do. I worry over Baby Earl. His brother Studs has taken to teasing Baby Earl because he don't talk. Last week, Studs hung Baby Earl upside down by his ankles and told him he'd stay that way until he cried, "Catfish." Baby Earl just hung there silent and so I pelted Studs with rotted sweet potatoes, which made him put Baby Earl down to chase after me. He didn't catch me because I can run faster than an October wind fussing up a storm.

I comfort myself now with the thought that Baby Earl and I will be together at dusk—at which time, if the cat's agreeable and shows me the way, I'll have saved Goodlow Pryce and I'll have that loving boy beside me.

I hurry downstairs wearing Goodlow's love-enchanted locket hidden under my dress and the cat soft with sleep slung in my arms just like he was a baby. I got to get this cat waked up and as anxious to go after Goodlow as I am.

Grandpa Stokes stands at our woodstove, rustling us up some *Poor-Do*, which is leftover corn bread fried in grease until crisp and it does taste good. Grandpa looks up from his frying pan, sees me with a cat and says, "Where'd that cat with them funny ears come from, Gnat? You steal it?"

"No, Grandpa, it fell out of the nighttime sky and I caught it." This is the truth and the truth makes Grandpa scratch his bald spot and look puzzled. His dog, that silly Ida Red who drools at Grandpa's side while angling for a bite of food, glances at the cat and me and she cocks her right ear.

"What were you doing outside after dark?" Grandpa asks me.

"I'd just stepped outside to show them Darnells how

pretty the moon was." I'm aiming for the truth and only missing by a hair. I can't let Grandpa know I was outside after dark—not after what I done and I won't do nothing like it ever again, I swear.

The cat noses my arm and so I set him down. The cat rubs up against Ida Red's front leg and this sets her lower jaw to quivering.

Grandpa Stokes and I watch Ida Red sniff the cat up his short full tail, which ain't polite and the cat bats her nose to tell her so. Then the cat pads over to our one rag rug and lies down in the center of it on his side. Using his forepaws, he inches his front end up until he's sitting on the curve of his backbone with his tail spread out before him and his two peaches proudly in full view. He places his front paws in his lap and stares at the cabin wall, which Grandpa has plastered with *Brownlow's Knoxville Whig* to keep out the wind. Grandpa Stokes taught me to read from that newspaper and now it looks like the cat's reading it, too.

"This cat ain't normal." Grandpa scratches his bald spot once again. "I declare, Gnat—this must be a Swamp Cat or Andrew Jackson ain't the first president of these United States who got himself born into a cabin!

"Gnat, how'd you end up with a Swamp Cat?" Grandpa's blue eyes stare into mine—I got me one brown eye and one pale green, which has led some to speculate that I might be part Swamp myself, which is ridiculous. If I was part Swamp, I'd have magical powers, which I don't.

The cat swivels his rounded head. Now he's gazing at me, too.

I take a good breath and I say, "Grandpa, this here Swamp Cat chose me to fall out of the sky to, because my heart is full of fire to save the world and be a hero!" I glance at the Swamp Cat, who didn't know this, but he does now. He shifts his gaze from me to a newspaper headline on the wall before him: *Our government is the greatest and the best the world has ever seen.*

Grandpa and I both love that government—long live the Union!

"You don't need to be no hero!" Grandpa says. "You need to keep yourself out of trouble—that is all!" He slams his hand against the table so hard, it scares Ida Red and she pees on the floor, but the cat don't move.

"We need us a teacher!" Grandpa grabs what he can to swipe up the pee—his flannel handkerchief. "We need us a teacher to keep your gnat-brain occupied so you don't go burning down no more tub mills like you did a week ago last Tuesday."

"I didn't mean to burn down that tub mill, you know that, Grandpa." I hate that he's brought this up. I hate that I burned down the only tub mill in Mary's Cove. Now we ain't got no way to grind our corn. Without ground corn, we can't make corn bread, cornmeal mush, flapjacks and pot likker dumplings. Hot tears flood my eyes.

"I warned you never to go anywheres near Foggy Bottom after dark," Grandpa says while wiping up pee. "I warned you and I warned you. But did you listen? No. And that poison mist there reached across the creek and worked its way into your brain. That mist said to you:

"See that pretty cobweb on the tub mill, Gnat? Wouldn't it look prettier if you set it on fire?"

Grandpa repeats the same words I told him a whispery Voice hidden inside the Foggy Bottom mist said. I never should have told Grandpa what that Voice said, but I was upset by what I'd done. I didn't know when I lit one cobweb thread that it would lead to another and another—causing the fire to spread through the entire workings of the tub mill! From the way the Voice cackled as I tried to fight the fiery blazes, I'm sure it did.

"I declare, Gnat Stokes. There are times I don't know what to do with you." Grandpa straightens up. He puts his hands on his bony hips and once more, I find him staring hard into my eyes.

"Don't send me to the Francis Spittle Home for Wayward Girls in Hell on Earth. Please, Grandpa." I'm told that home where DeWitt Lawson wants to send me is a terrible place where you sit all day and sew samplers for rich people. And if you dare to rest, that Francis Spittle pokes your eyes out with her knitting needles! "Just find me a teacher, Grandpa," I say. "One with lots of books for me to read and a patient heart to help me understand them. That way, I'll learn to do what's right and then, you'll see, I'll change our whole world for the better."

11

Over breakfast—that *Poor-Do* Grandpa has fried up and now softened with a tad of Ida Blue's rich cream—Grandpa calms down enough to ask if I know the Swamp Cat's true name, which I don't and I admit to Grandpa that I hadn't given it any thought. Grandpa says, "If you don't guess the cat's true name, by midnight tonight, them Swampers will take it back."

"Do you know this for a fact?" I ask.

"Course I do. I know more than a thing or two about them Swampers. You know that, Gnat." Grandpa looks at me with what seems like love and understanding in them pale blue eyes of his. I ain't never recognized this look in Grandpa's eyes. Is this the locket's doing? I ain't sure how to handle Grandpa's gaze, so I drop mine.

"How do I figure out a cat's true name?" I ask a spot of milk gravy on our red checkered tablecloth.

Grandpa says, "You look into the cat's big gold eyes and guess. If you guess right, I reckon the cat will let you know."

"How many guesses do I get?" I ask.

Grandpa says he reckons I get three. He says, "You got the day to think them over."

"The day? I ain't got the day!" I need to get this here cat named right now! I got to follow him to Goodlow!

"You've not only got the entire day; you've got until tonight at midnight. It's what we had when your pappy brought you home," Grandpa says.

Folks say it took clear up to midnight and all of Mary's Cove to name me right. That's because no one was quite sure who or what I was—not knowing my momma. Them fools thought I could be part Swamp! Folks kept guessing at my name—*May Bell, Lucille, Elizabeth Jane* . . . I'd whine and carry on. "She's a pesky little gnat," they'd say and pass me on to the next person. Each time they said *Gnat,* I got real quiet.

I love my Gnat name.

"Let's get on and eat this *Poor-Do,*" Grandpa says. "We got a mountain of chores waiting for us—including rebuilding the Drinkwaters' tub mill." Grandpa sets to eating his *Poor-Do* real calm-like, but from the way his wiry fingers grip his eating knife, I know I'd better be real careful with him.

I give him several quiet moments and then I say, "Grandpa, what if I don't guess the right name?" My heart throbs in my throat. If them Swampers take back the cat, how will I find my way to Goodlow?

Grandpa says he reckons since the Darnells was with

me when I caught the cat, they get some guesses. "How many guesses do the Darnells get?" I ask. Grandpa reckons they each get one. "What if the Darnells don't guess the right one? What do we do then?" I ask. Grandpa sighs and says he reckons, seeing as how the cat's staying in his cabin and reading his newspapers, Grandpa gets at least one guess.

"That's seven guesses. If that don't do it, I can bring in Granny Hart and Buffer McLeod to help us out," I say.

"I reckon you can," Grandpa says. "But an animal will tire after being hounded to death with name calling, Gnat. And then it might not answer even if someone does guess the right one. So if I was you, I wouldn't overdo it as you sometimes have a mind to." Grandpa pushes himself away from the table.

"But Grandpa, if it hears the right name—"

"Gnat Stokes, that's enough! I want no more questions put to me. All your questions make me itch!"

"Them questions will help me figure out how to keep a Swamp Cat!" I scream this so loud, Ida Red lets loose with what pee she has left and the cat leaves off reading the newspaper to watch her.

12

efore I attack my morning chores, I lock the Swamp Cat in the cabin and place my cross of nails above him on the fireplace mantelpiece. Even though them Swampers ain't known for coming out of Foggy Bottom in the daylight, still, this here cat might draw them out and I don't want them sneaking down the chimney to steal him in the middle of the afternoon!

I make sure the cat's comfortable with a bowl of cream for breakfast, a pan of dirt in which to tend to his necessaries and, of course, he's got all them newspapers on our walls to read. The passage he's looking at right now was writ by Parson Brownlow, who started the newspaper and he loves the Union:

" . . . I will muster men enough in the county where I reside, to hang the last rascal among you, and then use your carcasses for wolf-bait!"

Them rascals he's referring to are Rebels. The war may be over elsewhere, but here on the newspapered walls of my cabin, war is alive and kicking and it always will be! I leave the cat to read about it while I milk Ida

Blue. I feed her and our mule Ida Green their breakfast while thinking on a cat's true name and then I peek in the cabin window to make sure the cat's still there and to get some name inspiration from him.

The cat's lying on the rag rug with all four paws up in the air!

Have I kilt the cat? Somehow I have kilt the cat! I rush inside the cabin and that kilt cat with the four up-raised paws turns his head and he looks over at me real sleepy-like.

"You ain't dead," I tell him.

He blinks his big gold eyes at me.

"You ain't dead," I repeat. He blinks again. I scratch underneath them funny turned-down ears he's got. He seems to like it; he seems to want to purr but I think he don't know how. This makes me feel real sorry for him and here, he ain't got a heartbeat neither. His name could be *Purrless.* Or *Heartless.* Maybe I should call him *Ain't Dead Yet.*

I leave the cat to his peculiar sleeping style and go outside to gather eggs from every which place our hens choose to lay them while continuing to think on the cat's true name. The sun burns off the morning fog on our gentle slope with its meadow full of dry grass and blooming goldenrod. The cat's name could be *Golden-rod. . . .*

At the fence surrounding Grandpa's corn and bean

patch, I find me a brown egg next to Grandpa's big flat rock where we lay out our apples to dry in the sun. On this rock is a message writ in Grandpa's beans and it don't give me no name for a cat. This message ain't nice:

GNAT STOKES!

RETURN THE CAT OR I WILL RIP YOUR INSIDES OUT!

ZELDA

Them Swampers from the night before must have told Zelda I caught the cat and brought it to my cabin. Does she know I plan to follow the cat to Goodlow? Does she know I plan to save him from her? I bet she does. I bet she's got the all-overs from worrying about what I'm gonna do to her. I'm gonna steal her Goodlow!

I grab up Zelda's bean message so Grandpa Stokes won't see it. He'd have a conniption fit—me trucking with the Swamp Queen. He don't want me having nothing to do with her. He won't even let me peek out our front window at her and them Swampers when they parade through Mary's Cove on All Hallows' Eve! Grandpa sits on me the whole darn time. If Grandpa catches me trying to peer through the Foggy Bottom mist for a glimpse of a Swamper—even though I'm on our side of Tucker Creek—Grandpa tans me good.

He sure ain't fond of Swampers!

I look around for other signs that Zelda's been here

and I find them—panther paw-prints. They've cut themselves so deep into our meadow grass, you can see the poke marks of each sharp claw. I follow them paw-prints and as I do, I make sure to rub out each one I come upon with my bare feet. Them prints lead out from Grandpa's drying rock and to our cabin. They circle our cabin three times before finally giving up to head downhill toward Tucker Creek and beyond that to Foggy Bottom with its trees rising darkly from the mist, which, even with the sun now high in the sky, has not burned off and never will.

I ain't scairt of Zelda. I go about my chores hardly thinking of her creeping up behind my back to gut my bowel and leave it for the turkey buzzards to pick at. Still, in the afternoon, when Grandpa orders me to gather hickory nuts while he and his friend Buffer go on down to the Drinkwaters to help rebuild that tub mill, I do not insist they take me with them. That tub mill is too close to Foggy Bottom for my comfort. Besides which, Silas Drinkwater don't like me near his property; I worry him.

13

On the sunny ridge in back of our cabin, I gather hickory nuts while thinking on the cat's name. I hardly give a thought to Zelda creeping up behind me because the shagbark hickory ain't that far from Granny Hart's cabin. I feel safe near Granny's. She's a mountain granny woman—always doing things for others. She helped Grandpa by taking care of me until I was weaned from her nanny goat and I'd grown out of nappies.

Granny knows all sorts of things! How to make you feel better when you're sick by plumping your pillow just right. She makes the best biscuits. They don't crumble when you part them with a knife. She has cures for mosquito bites and poison ivy. She's real good at catching babies. She has the second sight and she's the keeper of our stories.

I hope that one day, I'll grow up to be a mountain granny woman just like her.

From listening to Granny, I've learned some interesting things about Zelda. Especially when Granny and Buffer, who came here from the Old Country, have a head-to-head about the Swamp Queen. This here's some of what I've learned:

1. The Swamp Queen ain't fond of preachers. Granny figures this is why Zelda didn't move here from the Gobbler's Glen side of Foggy Bottom until after them Rebels had done run off our Preacher John—him giving such loud and rousing sermons you could hear them clear across Mary's Cove and into the bottomland itself.

Now you may wonder, as many have, what drew the Swamp Queen to Mary's Cove to begin with. You may as well know right off—it wasn't me! My momma ain't that wicked Zelda—drawn here to keep a distant eye on a red-haired daughter she abandoned at birth. No sir. And if you meet up with a Vera May Clauser who tells you otherwise, she's lying.

2. Them Swampers all serve Zelda. She's their Dark Queen. Buffer thinks them Swampers followed Zelda to Foggy Bottom from the Old Country several hundred years ago. Living in the swamp has changed them. Where once, in the Old Country, you had shining knights in armor, in Foggy Bottom you got Swamp Knights covered with rust. Instead of a standing army, you got Warrior Bogies with catfish heads. As for fair-skinned court ladies in fancy dress, they're now pale green and I'm told they got black mold growing on their tattered gowns.

Zelda rules them all with the magic power of a cold

green ring she wears on the fourth finger of her right hand. She rules even them little Swamp Faeries in polka-dotted dresses that make them look like flutter-bys. Granny says Zelda's power ain't founded on love the way it should be, but on careless lust and greed, which is against the law and all teachings of the Bible.

3. To feed her greed, Zelda's working to overtake Mary's Cove and make it her own. Over the past year, she's had her Swampers throw buckets of mud into our Hallelujah Pond where Preacher John once saved the lives of infidels by baptizing them with total immersion. Our folk are too plumb tired from chores to try and clean out that mud. The pond's starting to fill in, although the middle continues to be real deep. Folks fear that slowly, slowly, with all the mud, the pond will turn to swamp. The swamp will grow bigger and bigger, the way swamps can and do. It'll overtake Mary's Cove—driving us out—and then Zelda will move in.

We got to drive out Zelda first!

4. The Dark Queen recruits human beings, whether they be alive like our Goodlow Pryce, or dead. That time Frank Gump and his Stuart Hollow Boys tried to ambush my grandpa and failed (Pappy wasn't riding with them—that time) Grandpa kilt them dead and they was buried. Zelda had their bones dug up. She turned Frank and his Boys into her skeleton crew. Buffer has seen them skeletons carrying pails of swamp mud across

Tucker Creek to the pond. Buffer says woe betide any of us mortals who gets in their way. Them Boys got fire burning out of their dark and empty eye sockets. They are mean and hungry.

But they don't bother me none. Why, if Zelda, her Swamp Knights, a hundred Warrior Bogies, a thousand pale green ladies and them skeletons, too—even that Foggy Bottom Swamp Guard, Jib's Boogety Bear— should come creeping up on me right now, I'd just holler and spit them in the eye. I have no care in the world except to gather hickory nuts and think on a cat's true name. Until a high-pitched voice right behind me says, "Howdy, Gnat!" Which makes me jump so fast and high, I almost lose my skin.

14

It's Penelope, that gal whose name is on the enchanted locket I wear beneath my dress and don't mean to take off no matter what. She's got her spotted dog with her. He stands loyally at her side—his hackles raised, ready and willing to defend her from me and here I'm two heads shorter than she is, seven years younger and I ain't threatened her or nothing. Although I did burn down her pappy's tub mill, for which I have apologized.

Penelope has always been right pretty and today, she looks prettier than ever even though she's getting up in years. Why, she must be near nineteen! She's got on a clean white blouse and a dark skirt, with a green cloak falling softly from her shoulders. Her blue eyes, peering close so's she can see me (as I said earlier, she's short-sighted), shine like stars, and her cheeks are flushed pink like someone, why, like someone who's in love.

"What are you doing clean up here?" I ask her.

"Visiting Granny Hart. She gave me a love charm." Penelope lowers her eyelids. "It's to keep away Studs Darnell. He stuck a dead squirrel in my apron strings and told me it was a marriage gift!" When Penelope looks up, her eyes sparkle with such fierceness, it almost blinds me. She says, "I threw that dead squirrel back at Studs, which Pappy says was wrong of me. Pappy says, 'Penelope, it's high time you stopped dreaming about Goodlow and get married.'

"Gnat, I'd kill myself before I'd marry Studs."

"What love charm did Granny give you to ward him off?" I hope it's a strong one. I may want Goodlow for my own, but I don't want Penelope to have to kill herself because she's about to be saddled with the meanest boy Mary's Cove has ever seen.

"Granny gave me a dead toad," Penelope says. "She fixed it so that to Studs, it will smell awful, and he won't come near me. But to anyone I like it'll smell sweet. I got it hanging from a string around my neck." Penelope places her hand over a lump beneath the front ruffle on her clean white blouse and I feel my face go hot. I have on a golden locket meant for her, she has on a toad.

"I will wear this toad until Goodlow and I reunite." She says this solemn, like a true love pledge. "Goodlow and I will reunite one day. Ain't we the pot of gold? You know that story, Gnat?"

"Course I know it." Granny's been telling it for over seven years. How there'd been a storm and then a warm sun, which brought out the first rainbow folks had ever seen in Mary's Cove. Folks found Goodlow sitting with

Penelope at the rainbow's end. Caught up in golden sunlight, they fed each other blackberries. Folks said, "If this pot of gold ain't a sign of good fortune for Mary's Cove, we don't know what is."

That rainbow shined after every rainfall—spring, summer and fall—for two years. And it always ended wherever Penelope and Goodlow happed to be outside together.

"I will always love Goodlow." Penelope reaches down and pets her dog. He kisses her hand with his pink tongue. He loves Penelope. Everyone loves Penelope.

I ain't giving up Goodlow on account of her.

"Gnat," Penelope says in a confiding tone, "today, at Granny's cabin, I met a stranger lady. Her name's Miss Hope and she's come to live with Granny. Miss Hope has got a gold tooth up top in her head and she's versed in love. I told her about Goodlow and how I hunger for his arms to hold me and do you know what Miss Hope said?" Penelope leans so close, I can smell the toad she wears. It smells sweet. Penelope likes me.

I don't like that she likes me.

"What did Miss Hope say?" I ask.

"Miss Hope said, 'Penelope, one day Goodlow will return to you. I feel it in my heart.'" Tears fill Penelope's eyes. Now why does she have to cry! I hate to see anyone cry! She says, "And then, that gold tooth of hers twinkled as if to say, *This is the gospel truth*."

"Well, I wouldn't go believing in a tooth," I say.

"I would! Miss Hope is real knowledgeable, Gnat. She's college educated and I know you're gonna love this next part." Penelope leans over so she can smile into my face with her even white teeth. "Miss Hope's brought a whole passel of books with her to Mary's Cove. Schoolbooks and the like. She's set on living with Granny Hart and rebuilding our school. She wants to be our teacher!"

"We're getting us a teacher?" This is the best news I've had all day!

"We are if DeWitt Lawson will allow it. You know how dead-set he is against education with its highfalutin ideas," she says.

"We need them ideas!" I grab up my basket. "We need us a teacher with highfalutin ideas more than anything! A teacher will open up our minds so that we can understand the world around us and learn to do what's right! That world is out there, Penelope, just waiting for us to seize and gobble it up!

"I'm off to meet Miss Hope." I head out for Granny's cabin with Penelope calling after me, "Don't burn down no more tub mills, Gnat."

"I won't!" Course I won't. I'm getting me a teacher. A teacher will keep my gnat-brain occupied. And she'll explain to me about mists and cobwebs and how they trick themselves right into the corner of a tub mill. And what those cobwebs are made of and what fire is and how it can consume a tiny thread—one tiny thread leading to another until you have a fiery conflagration.

A teacher can learn me about the Old Country with its queens and knights and courts. A teacher can help me settle on a Swamp Cat's true name! And then, once the cat's named and he's led me to Goodlow Pryce and I've gone and saved him from Zelda and he's my own true love, that teacher can help me to learn the true nature of life, and of love, so I won't get in trouble no more.

I need Miss Hope! Now!

15

Neither Granny Hart nor Miss Hope are at Granny's cabin by the time I get there, only the smoke left over from Granny's pipe and the old nanny goat I once nursed from when I was a baby. That goat never was too fond of me. Catching my scent, she hightails it around the cabin. I wonder where Granny is? She must have been called out to catch a baby and she took Miss Hope with her.

I peek in Granny's window for signs of the teacher woman with the gold tooth. The afternoon sun streams over my shoulder and pours its light on a green book set out on Granny's sewing table. Granny don't cotton much to books, so this must be Miss Hope's. It's got a gold circle on the cover and inside that circle are two gold words that sparkle in the sunlight just like they was writ in magic dust—*Little Women*.

Them two words are much nicer than the ones Zelda writ in beans on Grandpa's drying rock—GNAT! RETURN THE CAT OR I WILL RIP YOUR INSIDES OUT! My hands itch to grab hold of *Little Women* and take it home with me to read because I'm sure it's full of wise and loving words that can help me live my life. But I fight off the stealing urge because I know it ain't right to steal from someone who's a teacher.

Back home, them words *Little Women* dance inside my head just like they was Swamp Faeries holding hands in a circle while their little feet in golden slippers fly. I saw them faeries once. I tried to catch one, but she disappeared on me.

I reckon *Little Women* must hold some importance to me in my life. Maybe *Little Women* is the Swamp Cat's true name! It'd be just like Zelda—giving the name *Little Women* to a male cat so proud of his peaches, he likes to show them off. I study the cat, who's reading a section of Parson Brownlow's newspaper directly above Grandpa's musket that's propped next to his spittoon:

The Confederate kennel is now unloosed: all the pack—from the deep-mouthed bloodhound of South Carolina and Florida to the growling cur of Georgia—are baying at me.

"You'd better watch out for that brawling pack of Rebel hound dogs," I tell the cat.

He yawns at me. And then, that fool Swamp Cat, who, if I can get him named right, is supposed to lead me to the boy I love, falls over backward like he's been shot.

16

By the time them Darnells come running up the cabin path for supper, the cat's back on his feet, I've settled on my three names for him and the sun's sinking behind Old Baldy Top. Foggy Bottom, sprawling at the mountain's base, has turned blacker than pitch. The wind, blowing off that dark swampland, has picked up something fierce. It reminds me that All Hallows' Eve is coming on soon. The wind blows leaves into my face as Wanda, followed by Jib and Baby Earl, runs up the three porch steps to where I'm stacking kindling for the woodstove.

"Where's Goodlow?" Wanda pants into my face.

"He ain't here." As I go to explain to them Darnells about what's happened and how we got to name the cat, the wind kicks up such a fuss, I can't hear a word I say. So I lead everyone inside the cabin to talk and the wind slams the door behind Baby Earl, which causes him to jump the way I did earlier at the shagbark hickory. Grabbing up Baby Earl, I hug him hard. "Baby Earl? Did Studs leave you alone today?"

Baby Earl shakes his head, no.

"Baby Earl, you got to learn to talk! If you talk, you can put that stinky-eyed Studs in his place and he won't bother you no more! Besides which, I need your help.

"We got us a Swamp Cat here," I tell all three Darnells. "Grandpa says if we don't guess the cat's rightful name by midnight, we'll lose him!"

Baby Earl's lower lip starts in to quiver. I recall how them two slept so close together, I couldn't tell where the cat ended and Baby Earl began.

"You love that cat, don't you, Baby Earl," I say.

He nods real solemn-like.

I know just how he's feeling. Ain't I in love, too? If I lose that love, I don't know what I'll do. And here, I don't even really know him yet.

"Gnat? Who we gonna lose the Swamp Cat to?" Wanda says.

"Zelda. She wrote to me that she'd rip my insides out if I don't return her cat. But don't tell Grandpa. He don't know the Swamp Queen herself is involved." I glance over at him, rustling up some beans for supper. "Don't you mention Goodlow neither."

Wanda sucks in her breath and then, she sneezes. Whenever I got Wanda doing something for me she thinks she shouldn't, she sneezes. If Wanda could sell them sneezes, I swear she'd be rich.

Grandpa bangs his spoon on the supper pot. "Supper's ready! Come and get it and no cat naming until you clean your plate!"

While the cat cleans himself on Grandpa's rag rug and Ida Red snores beneath the table, we eat our beans. Grandpa explains to us about how many name guesses we each get, and why, and if we guess the right name, Grandpa reckons we'll so astound the cat, he'll break right down and purr.

"This cat don't know how to purr," I say, but I don't tell Grandpa I've already settled on my three names.

"Well then, I reckon the cat will meow," Grandpa says.

"He don't know how to do that neither," I say.

"Do you know this for a fact?" he says.

"I ain't heard him meow the whole time he's been here," I say.

"That don't mean he can't." Grandpa looks like he don't want me to pursue this no longer, so I don't, although it bothers me. How can the cat tell us we've guessed the right name if he can't meow? Grandpa says to them Darnells, "Be real thoughtful in your name choice. You only get one each."

As they eat their beans, Wanda and Jib furrow their foreheads in deep thought. Meanwhile, Baby Earl folds his hands on the table and studies the cat, now sitting on the rag rug with his head half-cocked.

Does the cat hear what I think I now hear—Zelda hissing in the night wind—"*Where'ssss my Swamp Cat?*"

No one seems to hear her but the cat and me.

"Grandpa Stokes, you did say we have 'til midnight to name the Swamp Cat," I say.

"I did. That's the rule and if folks say different, they're lying." Grandpa now studies Baby Earl, who studies the cat, who's still got his head cocked—

"Where'ssss my cat?"

It'd be just like Zelda to break a rule. I reckon she thinks with that magic ring she's got, she has the right to break anything. She's a wicked, wicked Swamp Queen.

"Baby Earl?" Grandpa says. "You ain't but eaten two spoonfuls of your supper. To grow up big and strong, you've got to eat more beans."

"Eat more beans," I tell Baby Earl so as to cover up Zelda's hiss, growing ever closer—*"Where'ssss my cat?"*

"Grandpa Stokes? I think we should name the Swamp Cat now," I say.

"Not until Baby Earl eats his beans!" Grandpa slams his hand on the table. "That boy needs to eat his beans so that he can grow up strong—like General Ulysses S. Grant!"

Baby Earl grins and shovels a spoonful of beans into his mouth. He shovels in another. Zelda's hiss grows closer yet and still, nobody seems to hear her but the cat and me.

I shout to drown out Zelda and encourage Baby Earl

to eat: "Beans, beans, the musical fruit. The more you eat, the more you toot. The more you toot, the better you feel, so eat more beans at every meal."

"Eat more beans!" Wanda shouts.

"Eat more beans!" Jib shouts.

"I WANT MY SWAMP CAT!" Zelda shrieks.

And everybody stops dead.

17

Zelda's shriek now causes poor Wanda to sneeze up a fit, Jib to wail and Ida Red to bark. Barking, that fool dog hurls herself at our front door like she was a match for Zelda, which she ain't. "Rebel bushwhackers!" Grandpa shouts and reaches for his musket.

I shout, "Don't shoot, Grandpa! Don't shoot! It's Zelda. You shoot Zelda, she'll multiply!"

"That's Zelda?" Grandpa shrieks.

"We've got to name the cat!" I throw myself on the floor in front of him. "We've got to name him NOW!" The cat stares at me with big gold eyes. I say softly now so as not to frighten him, "Cat, your name is Goldenrod."

The cat don't show no sign of recognition.

I try again, "Cat, your name is Peaches!"

That don't work neither.

"Well then, cat," I say, "I reckon your name is Little Women."

The cat stares so hard at me, I fear his eyeballs are about to burst. Outside, Zelda hisses—"*Cat'ssss mine.*"

She presses her face against our window. She's changed herself into a panther. I reckon she thinks that with her evil pale green panther eyes, white dripping fangs and tongue the color of the insides of a chicken gizzard, she can scare us into giving up the cat. I scream at her, "He ain't yours yet!"

The cat gets to his feet. He heads toward our supper table, tail held high. Wanda stops her sneezing to call out, "Cat, your name is King!"

The cat keeps right on walking.

Jib calls out, "Cat, your name is Poison Fang!"

The cat circles Grandpa's chair.

Grandpa shouts, "Cat, your name is Ida Gray."

The cat leaps onto the supper table. He sits himself down next to Baby Earl's plate that had been full of beans but is almost empty now. The cat stares hard at Baby Earl. Baby Earl stares hard right back.

At the window, Zelda moans.

Grandpa Stokes yells at her, "Stop your bellyaching!" Which surprises me and yet, it don't. When it comes to protecting family, friends and little creatures, my grandpa will stand up to anyone. And I . . . I love him for it.

Grandpa turns to Baby Earl. In a voice grown softer and more gentle-like, Grandpa says to the little boy, "All right, General Grant, it's time for you to speak up."

And do you know what that little general does? In a

sweet high voice I have never before heard, he says, "Eat more beans."

"Baby Earl, that ain't no cat's name!" Wanda shrieks.

"At least Baby Earl tried." I pet him on the head while trying to be proud of him for talking, and holding back my tears. I ain't never gonna get to Goodlow now.

"Eatmore Beans," Baby Earl says.

"Eatmore Beans?" I say.

"Eatmore Beans?" Jib and Wanda say.

The cat opens his mouth like he's trying to meow, only it comes out as a squeak.

"The cat's name is Eatmore Beans!" I scream.

18

There ain't nothing like the power of love. Because of it, we got a wordless boy talking and a meowless cat squeaking. Baby Earl's done named the Swamp Cat and now that little boy holds the cat named Eatmore Beans in his arms. The cat licks a spatter of beans off Baby Earl's chin. Them two belong together—same as Goodlow Pryce and me.

At the window, Zelda sets into caterwauling fit to die! She can't take back her Swamp Cat now! He'll lead me to Goodlow! I grab up Baby Earl along with the cat and I cover Baby Earl's round face with kisses.

"Hooray for General Grant!" Grandpa does a little jig. Jib grabs Wanda's hands and they dance together across the floor. I swirl with Baby Earl, cradling the cat. We have us a dancing celebration until, all of a sudden-like, Zelda stops her caterwauling and everything goes real quiet. All you can hear is the fire popping in the woodstove.

Grandpa Stokes says, "Something don't feel right."

Grandpa goes over to our one front window and

looks out. "I don't see Zelda nowhere." Grandpa sniffs the air. Grandpa says, "Zelda's gone, but I smell something she's left behind.

"By gum!" he says. "That Zelda's done gone and sprayed our cabin with her scent! Pure panther. She's marked our cabin for her Warrior Bogies!"

"Them bogies will sniff their way here while we're sleeping!" Jib cries out as I catch Zelda's scent, sharp enough to make your eyes tear. "They'll hump their way up the back steps," Jib says. "They'll wrap their tentacles around our heads! They'll suck out everything we got—brains, eyeballs, spit."

"We got to stop them!" Wanda shouts.

"Gnat Stokes?" Grandpa glares at me. "You got us into this situation. How in tarnation do you suppose you're gonna get us out?"

"Give me a moment to think on it." I put down Baby Earl with his cat. I need to think on this real hard. If them Warrior Bogies come out the way Grandpa says, there'll be no getting past them to follow Eatmore Beans to Goodlow.

What to do? I pace back and forth as I try to work it out. I got to do something. I can't let Zelda's Warrior Bogies spell the end of all my love and hero plans.

19

It don't take me long to figure out the means by which to solve our bogie problem—Grandpa's hidden cache of moonshine. All we got to do is pour Grandpa's moonshine wherever Zelda sprayed. That potent moonshine will cover Zelda's scent so them bogies can't follow it to Grandpa's cabin through that front tentacle of theirs, which, I'm told, not only can sting you blind, but also doubles as a nose. If we are fortunate, and sometimes we are, by tomorrow morning, the moonshine and panther scent will have evened each other out so you won't smell nothing—nothing at all! And me? I'll be on my way to Goodlow.

"Having moonshine is against the law in Mary's Cove. I'll be thrown in jail if DeWitt Lawson catches wind of it," Grandpa mutters as he takes out several jugs of that moonshine from his secret place beneath our cabin floor.

"Then, let's pray there ain't no wind," I say.

So we do and later when we step outside (all except our hero Baby Earl, who stays inside, loving Eatmore

Beans the way I yearn to be loving Goodlow—hugging him hard) we discover our prayers have been answered. That nasty wind, which, earlier, had been attacking me with leaves, has died and where Zelda once had shrieked, little cicadas now call back and forth: *shieka-kiecka-zzzzt. Shieka-kiecka-zzzzt.*

We sprinkle moonshine on the front porch, the three porch steps, around the cabin and down our path. Provided the moonshine fools them bogies and Eatmore Beans does what he should, I'll be following him down the path and into Foggy Bottom at dawn tomorrow—October 30th, the day before All Hallows' Eve. Wish I could leave sooner, but as desperate as I am for going after Goodlow, there ain't no way I can see to follow after a gray cat in the dark.

20

Once the moonshine's done poured out, and I'm about to follow Wanda and Jib back inside the cabin, Grandpa stops me on the porch. Grandpa says, "Gnat, I've got my suspicions. My suspicions tell me there's more to what's been going on here than your wanting to name and keep the Swamp Cat.

"What are you up to?" He squints his eyes like he's trying to look inside my heart.

"I ain't up to nothing, Grandpa," I say with as much honesty as I can muster. If Grandpa knew all that I was up to, he'd lock me up in DeWitt Lawson's cold cellar that doubles as a jailhouse and swallow the key.

Later, Grandpa takes them Darnells aside. While I clean up from supper, he has a head-to-head talk with them over by his spittoon. I know they're talking about me and what I'm up to by the way Jib, Wanda and Baby Earl keep glancing in my direction.

If them Darnells tell Grandpa about my planning to go after Goodlow, I'll skin them alive!

Now, up in my loft, they're bunched together like a

patch of wild onions (the cat still in Baby Earl's arms). They whisper among themselves as I bring out *Ten Nights in a Bar-Room* from underneath my corn shuck mattress. Grandpa's got them Darnells plotting against me.

I set to reading silently and to myself.

After a while, that Wanda, she clears her throat and she says, "Gnat?"

I look up to find all three Darnells lined up in front of me. The cat sits in Baby Earl's arms. The cat regards me with his big gold eyes. Wanda, her thin face now bright pink, says, "Gnat, we want to tell you something we got planned and you can't talk us out of it, you hear?"

I don't say nothing.

"It starts with Ma in the corn patch." Wanda's always one for starting in a corn patch. "We'll be out picking ears like today—Ma keeping her hawk eye on us young 'uns. All of a sudden, Jib will start thinking on boiled squirrel with cold white gravy."

Jib slaps her hand to her mouth like she's gonna be sick.

"Don't think on it now!" Wanda and I both shriek.

Holding her hand to her mouth, Jib turns her skinny back on us and Wanda says, "As I said, Jib will think on something that will make her throw up everything she ate for breakfast. I'll take her to the cabin like I always do when Jib makes herself sick. I'll fix her spicewood tea. Baby Earl, as always, will come along.

"Instead of going to our cabin, we'll come to yours.

"Gnat." Wanda leans into me. "Us Darnells can't let you follow Eatmore Beans to Goodlow Pryce all on your own. What if the Swamp Cat leads you into Foggy Bottom?"

"The Swamp Queen's there," Jib says. "Your grandpa says she'll eat you alive."

"If you've told Grandpa I'm going after Goodlow—"

"We didn't tell him, Gnat, I swear." Wanda don't sneeze so I reckon she's being truthful. She says, "He's just worried about you, is all. He don't like you fooling around with Foggy Bottom. He says it's real dangerous for you. He says if you make the mistake of going in there, you might never come back out. And then we'd never see you again.

"Gnat." Wanda draws in her breath. When she lets it out, the following words come with it—"We're going after Goodlow with you so that we can protect you. We'll get to you by noon tomorrow. I swear."

Noon tomorrow? But time's so short. I need to be off by dawn!

Wanda goes on. "Since Baby Earl named the cat, Baby Earl will take the lead in following him wherever he might lead—even into Foggy Bottom. Jib and I, carrying sticks, will march on either side of you. Zelda's got

them Warrior Bogies for her army. You got us Darnells—all three." Wanda sticks out her pointed chin,
raises her right hand and she salutes me.

"We'll march with you come what may—Warrior
Bogies, Swamp Knights, even Boogety Bears," Jib says.

"We'll march with you to Hell and Beyond," Wanda
says.

"Me, too," Baby Earl says.

"I appreciate that," I tell all three.

And I do. Here I thought my friends had betrayed
me to my grandpa and instead, I got me a Darnell
Army! And even if I don't call up that army to aid me
in my mission, still, its steadfast loyalty and devotion to
my cause does bring to mind Granny Hart's love crystal, with each of its sparkling and precious sides.

I love them Darnells.

21

In bed, Eatmore Beans drapes himself over Baby Earl's stomach while I read to my army—*Ten Nights in a Bar-Room*, "Night the Second," in which Joe Morgan's little girl Sarah gets hit in the head with an empty drinking glass and is stunned into insensibility. In the middle of the most exciting part, Baby Earl speaks for the fifth time in what I believe must be his entire life. Baby Earl says, "Don't like it."

"You don't like *Ten Nights in a Bar-Room*?" I ask.

"Don't like it," Baby Earl repeats.

"Baby Earl, we need to find out what happens to little Sarah," I say.

That lip of Baby Earl's starts to quiver.

"Baby Earl, it's the only adventure book we got!"

"Gnat's right, Baby Earl," Wanda says.

"I like *Ten Nights*," Jib says. "Troubles mount. Situations grow worse and worse."

Baby Earl's lip quivers ever harder. He's going to cry. I can't let our little general cry! I say, "Baby Earl! I tell you what! Since you bravely named the cat even while

Zelda shrieked her tonsils out, we'll forget *Ten Nights* this evening and recite instead your favorite poem by Robert Burns—'My Heart's in the Highlands.'"

Baby Earl's lip stops quivering altogether and I pull Wanda and Jib to their feet. As Eatmore Beans and Baby Earl look on, the Darnell gals join hands with me in a circle. We jump up and down on my corn shuck mattress and we shout:

My heart's in the Highlands, my heart is not here;
My heart's in the Highlands a-chasing the deer;
Chasing the wild deer, and following the roe,
My heart's in the Highlands wherever I go.

We shout our way through Baby Earl's favorite poem three times and then, we all flop down and that's when I tell them Darnells about Miss Hope. "She wants to be our teacher! She's got books from which to teach us, including one that looks real interesting to me— *Little Women.*"

"*Little Women?*" Jib flops onto her stomach, looks sideways at me and says, "Ain't *Little Women* one of them names you tried on Eatmore Beans?"

"Yes it is, Jib. And I meant no disrespect by it." I look at Eatmore Beans, who sits on the quilt square that should have my momma's name writ on it, but it don't. "*Little Women* is the name of a book and there ain't nothing wrong with a book!" I tell the cat. "A book can take you into worlds you ain't never seen. A book can lead you on exciting adventures. A book can say, 'Hey, you ain't alone in the world. Look here. In these pages, you'll find someone who's just like you and going through what you are—good and bad.'"

The Swamp Cat, who's fond of reading himself (don't he read our newspapers?), nods his head in agreement and then he blinks his big gold eyes at me.

22

Goodlow's enchanted locket continues to work its spell on me even as I sleep. Sleeping, I dream once more that I'm with that precious boy in his prison cave somewhere deep inside Old Baldy Top Mountain. In this dream, Goodlow holds me in his arms so that my heart and his, they beat as one. His skin is as soft as warm night air and he smells like crushed mint leaves. I hope I smell as good to him. Holding me close in his strong arms, he says softly in my ear, "Follow the cat. Cat knows the way to me. Hurry!"

I wake up. It's the middle of the night. Eatmore Beans licks a dirt spot on my right arm. He's trying to clean me up. I hate to be cleaned up!

"Eatmore Beans! Go to sleep." I place him on top of Baby Earl. Baby Earl puts his arm over the cat and Eatmore Beans chatters his teeth at him—just like he's talking to the little boy. I turn away from them two.

Facing Wanda and her snores, I drift off. Again, I'm with Goodlow. He cradles my face in his large and gentle hands. With eyes that are so full of love for me it makes me want to cry, he tells me I am the prettiest gal in the world. I want to ask him if I'm as pretty as Penelope, but I'm afraid of what the answer might be and so I don't. He runs his fingers back from my forehead and through my long red hair. He whispers, "Cat knows the way to me. Hurry."

I wake up; it's still dark. The cat picks at my matted hair, like he's trying to comb it out with his teeth! I hate to have my hair combed! "Stop that, Eatmore Beans!" I place him on top of Baby Earl again. The little boy hugs the cat. Eatmore Beans chatters to him.

Baby Earl whispers: "She ain't gonna like it."

I can't be bothered with what I ain't gonna like. I need to get back to Goodlow. I drift off, hoping to find him once more in my dreams so I can tell him, "I'll be with you shortly." But this time I don't find him nowhere. I wake up at dawn feeling sad and full of longing to be with him. Baby Earl, already dressed and ready for the day, stands before me with Eatmore Beans slung in his arms and a sister on either side.

"Gnat?" Baby Earl looks like he's got something real important to say to me.

"Baby Earl. You have words. Use them words!" I say, and that little boy says, "Last night, Eatmore Beans said he won't lead you to Goodlow Pryce until you take a bath."

"I hate baths!" I say.

"Gnat hates Granny Hart's scalding water," Jib goes on for me. She licks her lips and says, "Gnat hates Granny's scrub brush that rips her flesh to the bone. Gnat hates Granny's lye soap that burns her eyeballs to a crisp."

"I hate it all." I eye the fool cat who brought up the bath subject to begin with. He gazes lovingly up at Baby Earl, who holds him just like he was his baby.

I want Goodlow Pryce to be holding me this way.

Will I ever get to him?

Standing before the little boy who not only named the Swamp Cat but now he's got the cat talking to him, I place my right hand over the golden locket I wear that holds Goodlow's message—*Cat nos the way 2 me. I luv u, Goodlow*—and say, "But to save Goodlow Pryce, I'll face scalding water, stinging lye soap and the brutal lash of the scrub brush. I'll do that and anything else this mission might require of me."

23

Them Darnells run off into the morning, leaving Eatmore Beans in our cabin to rest up for his journey and me to have a bath. Meanwhile, last night's adventures must have plumb wore out my grandpa. He's usually up by now and here he is, snoring with Ida Red alongside him, her head resting on his stomach. When I slip outside the cabin, I discover that the air's real still. There ain't no wind to broadcast the stench of moonshine mixed with panther spray that hangs over our cabin like a fog.

Until the sun burns off the fog, that pesky wind had better not show up to blow the smell of moonshine into DeWitt Lawson's hatchet face. The last time it did, DeWitt threw Grandpa Stokes in jail! Grandpa stayed in jail a week. He nearly suffocated from the dander which DeWitt's scalp gives off like snow spilling from a winter sky. Grandpa says DeWitt throws that dander in the jail cell for his prisoners to use as bedding while calling down to them, "Waste not, want not."

Grandpa said, "Whenever DeWitt said, 'Waste not, want not,' I'd cover my head."

I reckon we've wasted a ton of moonshine fooling Zelda's Warrior Bogies! I light out for Granny's, my bare feet pounding through leaf litter. In my rush, I almost bump into Vera May Clauser's old milk cow, no doubt out to find herself some mushrooms. That cow's real fond of mushrooms. That time I found her with her head stuck in a pail of mushrooms I'd just gathered, I freed her and led her home to Vera May. For three days afterward, that cow gave bubble milk. And do you know who Vera May blamed all them bubbles on? Me! She said I'd cast a spell on her cow's milk! She called me a Swamp Witch!

Everyone knows eating mushrooms will gas up a cow's milk good. Vera May's a fool! I swat her cow on its fat rump and hurry on my way. When I arrive at Granny's cabin, she's already up and out on her front porch, cutting up old sheets to make nappies for them babies she catches. That Granny! She's always practicing a side of love she calls doing good for others.

I say to her, "Granny, I've come for a scrub!" And she says, "Lordy sakes, Gnat Stokes, and here it ain't been three months since the last one. Have you come into puberty?"

"Granny Hart," I say as forthrightly as I can muster,

"puberty's done clobbered me hard. My head's spinning from it and my heart's on fire."

Granny leans down from her considerable height to peer into my face. I drop my gaze. I don't want Granny with her second sight to look in my eyes and see Goodlow in my heart. I feel Granny's strong hand rub itself along the top of my back and then latch itself onto my right shoulder. She says, "Come on inside, Gnat. I'll scrub you clean as God's right hand. But first, there's someone real special I want you to meet.

"Gnat, I've found you a teacher."

In her cabin, Granny introduces me to that teacher—Miss Hope! She's as tall and large-boned as Granny herself, but while Granny is old, Miss Hope is young. And while Granny has white hair, which she keeps tightly pulled back in a bun, Miss Hope's wild dark hairs spring forth from her head like a bunch of curly snakes which she's tried to pin down proper-like into a bun but it ain't working.

I pump the hand she offers me.

As Granny draws out her washtub in which to scrub me raw, I say to Miss Hope, "You ever read that book—*Little Women*?" I glance at it, sitting open on the sewing table like it was an invitation for me to steal it.

"I'm reading it right now," she says.

"What's it about?" I ask.

"Life and love." She smiles real broad-like and that gold tooth Penelope spoke of sparkles at me.

"I'm real interested in love." I glance at Granny to see what her reaction might be because I ain't never expressed no interest in love no matter how long and hard Granny has preached to me about it.

Granny's smiling.

"I'm partial to love myself," Miss Hope says.

"Do you like to read?" she says.

"I love to read," I say.

Miss Hope's face lights up like a jack-o'-lantern. This, along with her snake-like hair and her gold tooth, makes her real appealing to me. She says, "You can borrow *Little Women* from me when I'm done."

"I can?" Ain't no one ever lent me a book.

"I'll lend you *Little Women* and other books besides." Miss Hope points to Granny's corner cupboard where Granny stores her scrub brushes, combs, stinging lye soap, drawing powder for clogged pores and that smelly ointment which she smears on my skin to keep wood ticks from sucking me dry. Two whole shelves of that cupboard are now filled with books, while Granny's supplies spill out of a large oak basket on the floor.

"You got books in there that talk of the Old Country with its knights, queens and tiny faeries?" I ask Miss Hope. She nods.

"What about cobwebs, tub mills and fire?"

"I have books about them. I have history books, nature books, fairy-tale books, math books, geography books, poetry books—I have books about anything you can think of," she says.

"Ain't that nice." It's more than nice. It's getting me so excited, I can't barely stand myself. I've been waiting for a teacher all my life and here she is and with a stack of books that will open up the world to me! She even has poetry books! I'm partial to poetry. I can rhyme real good—sat, cat, Jehosephat!

She says, "I even have a book of Latin."

"What's Latin?" I say.

"It's our mother tongue," she says.

"Tell Gnat them three Latin words you taught me," Granny calls over to us. "They're magic words, Gnat. Miss Hope says if you have something hard to face, say the words aloud to yourself and they'll help to get you through it."

"What are them words?" I ask Miss Hope.

"*Amor Vincit Omnia,*" she says.

"What do they mean?" I say.

"Love Conquers All," she says.

"*Amor Vincit Omnia!*" I like the sound of them three Latin words. I reckon I'll find good use for them. They do sound magical to me.

24

Now, Granny Hart has three sermons in her and she always gives them to me as she holds me captive in her washtub. Today, I sit in hot water with knees pressed to my chest to cover the locket I've turned down so no one can see the name *Penelope* writ on it and Granny launches into her first sermon—that being "Cleanliness Is Next to Godliness." Granny has her gradations of cleanliness and she always starts me at the lowest rung—that being fodder for the devil's herd. As she scrubs the flesh off me, she slowly moves me up her celestial ladder until I'm scrubbed as clean, raw and honorable as one of them archangels sitting at God's right hand.

Granny's second sermon has to do with the talents; we got to make good use of our talents. Today, Granny pronounces her talent sermon as she works at the dirt behind my ears and Miss Hope attacks the grit beneath the nails of my right hand after rubbing some sweet-smelling violet water all through my hair.

"Gnat has many talents," Granny tells Miss Hope.

"She's good with fancy words. She can come up with words I ain't never heard of. And she's real smart. If she could think with her heart as well as her head, she could grow up to be a granny woman."

"Granny Gnat," I say, which causes Miss Hope to look up from my gritty fingernails and smile into my eyes. I've been so caught up in Miss Hope's snake-like hair, gold tooth and all them books she's got, I ain't noticed her eyes. They're the same color as our mountain mist—a smoky gray-blue.

As I'm looking at those eyes, Granny says, "Gnat, I've been noticing a gold locket you have on. Where'd it come from?"

Too flustered to lie, I say, "From a boy I love."

"You're in love?" Granny says.

"Yes, Granny, I am," I say.

"Well, praise be!" Granny says, at which point I expect her to launch into her third and final sermon— that being "The Many-Sided Crystal Called Love." But I reckon Granny's just too excited about my being in love to give me her sermon about it. Instead, she says, "Gnat, I have a dress I've been saving to give to you!"

Now, you got to understand, I already got two dresses. One is to wear while the other's being washed. Granny made them both for me out of pink flowered feed sacks. So wait 'til you hear what Granny brings out of her old wardrobe and puts on me after I've been scrubbed to Godliness and smelling sweet as violets. A dress the likes of which I have never before seen! It's cotton soft with gold threads worked through the pale white background and there's all these flowers on it that match the red in my hair. Only Miss Hope don't call my hair red. She calls it auburn. She says, "Gnat, you have such beautiful *auburn* hair."

In my new dress, I reach up to touch that hair—wild as always, bushing out from my head like mountain myrtle and smelling sweet. I say to Miss Hope, "We should pin my hair up—like yours."

"You ain't a grown woman like Miss Hope!" Granny says. "Gnat, you're a young gal. Let your hair hang free." Before I can think to glance away, her eyes burn into mine. For a single second, I see Goodlow Pryce reflected in Granny's eyes. That boy holds out his arms to me.

Granny pulls me away from Miss Hope. Granny takes me outside onto her front porch, where the wind is now whipping up a storm. When did the wind pick up? That wind smells of moonshine! I'd better warn Grandpa!

Granny says, "Gnat, I seen a full-grown enchanted boy inside your heart."

Too stunned to deny it, I nod.

"He ain't your boy! He's Penelope's!" Granny says.

I don't say nothing.

"Lordy sakes, Gnat! You're trucking where you don't belong!" she says.

"I'm trucking where I do belong! I'm trucking with love." In my red flowered dress and with my sweet hair flying free and auburn, I race away from Granny and into the pesky wind. I skirt Granny's old nanny goat; she bleats as Granny calls out to me over and over again, "Stop, Gnat. Stop!"

25

I don't stop running until I reach Grandpa's cabin and then, its stillness stops me dead. I don't hear no snores. There ain't no smoke rising from the chimney. When I call out, "Howdy!" Ida Red don't come barking out to greet me. I run alongside the silent cabin and up the front porch steps. On the outside of the front door is nailed an official-looking note writ in DeWitt Lawson's scrawl:

Arrested: Nathaniel Stokes
Crime: Harboring illegal moonshine
Trial: Noon, October 31st
Place: First Baptist Church
Bail: A hundred dollars

DeWitt Lawson must have smelt moonshine on the wind. He's arrested Grandpa!

Here I done caught me a Swamp Cat, got him named, used up most of Grandpa's moonshine to fool Zelda's Warrior Bogies, and had myself a bath—all so I could follow Eatmore Beans to my true love. And now Grandpa's been arrested and it's all my fault! I can't go off saving Goodlow with Grandpa suffocating in DeWitt Lawson's cold cellar on account of what I've done. But where can I find me a hundred dollars to free my grandpa? I ain't got a penny to my name!

I push open the cabin door. The main room's empty except for Eatmore Beans, who sits on his backside and chatters at a pile of dander next to Grandpa's spittoon. Grandpa must have really gotten DeWitt's dander up. He's left behind a pile of dead white skin flakes so big, it's enough to fill a tin cup.

Eatmore Beans takes one look at me and runs out the door that I left open.

I can't let this cat get away from me.

"Eatmore Beans!" I run after him and he tears away—skittering across the front porch, down the steps, past our bean shed, through our wind-whipped meadow and down, down toward Tucker Creek and Foggy Bottom. He's leading me to Foggy Bottom and I ain't ready to go there yet. I ain't got my cross of nails, nor moonshine neither. Grandpa's in jail!

"Eatmore Beans! You got to stop!" I scream.

Eatmore Beans slinks down until he's almost blended with a tall patch of timothy grass and he scurries onward. He leaps over a pile of windfall. I leap over it, too. I follow Eatmore Beans onto the big scaly trunk of a sycamore that's fallen dead across Tucker Creek near where Piney Gap Road fords it and DeWitt Lawson has posted his sign—Keep Out! This Means You!

Sitting on my bottom, I hitch myself along the tree trunk after the cat, who can move faster than I can because he don't have on a dress that keeps snagging up on branches.

I'm near three quarters across Tucker Creek and nearing the Foggy Bottom side—hoary with mist—when all of a sudden, tree branches, which had seemed normal-like, but snaggy on the Mary's Cove side, spring to life. Before I can think to jump off the tree and into the creek below, them branches whip themselves around me; they lash me tight to the tree trunk.

The tree's made a prisoner out of me!

"Eatmore Beans!" I scream.

He leaps off the prison tree and onto a dark boulder. He sits himself down on that boulder jutting out into the creek—not all that far from me. He puts his paws in his lap and says right out loud, "You're not Penelope."

"I know I ain't!" I can't believe a cat just talked to me and I talked back. It must have something to do with his being on the Foggy Bottom side of Tucker Creek and my being almost there.

"It's Penelope I'm supposed to be leading to the good lad," Eatmore says.

"Penelope's too shortsighted to save Goodlow! Only I can." I struggle to free myself from tree branches hugging the life out of me. They just hug me harder.

"Eatmore Beans?" I say as gentle as a tree prisoner can who's talking to a Swamp Cat. *I'm talking to a cat!* "How can I get this here tree to let me go?"

"Perhaps it's not meant to let you go." He lifts one paw and licks the bottom of it with his pink tongue. I'm a tree prisoner and he's giving himself a bath! I wish Baby Earl were here to talk to him for me. The cat says, "Then again, perhaps it is. Recite a bad poem, lassie, and we'll see."

"If I say a bad poem, this here swamp tree will let me go?" I want to make sure I got this right. It sounds awful easy and the swamp tree's gripping me real hard.

"Aye, lassie, it will. Do you have the talent for it?" Eatmore says.

"I like to rhyme words, so I reckon I do." It don't take but a moment for a bad poem to come to me and I say it real loud so the swamp tree will hear:

> I ain't never gonna be
> As bad or ugly as this here swamp tree,
> A tree whose snarly branches press,
> Me, Gnat Stokes, against its hoar-
>   struck chest.

I'm a poet, don't it see?
I can spout bad poems into eternity.
With a—

That's as far as I get; with a hiss and a whip, them snarly branches let me go. I fall off the tree and into Tucker Creek on my back. Rapids carry me downstream past Eatmore Beans on his rock and it takes some real doing on my part to finally swim myself over and around creek boulders to the misty Foggy Bottom side. I climb the bank.

I'm on the Foggy Bottom side of Tucker Creek for the first time since I was born. The Foggy Bottom mist wraps damp arms around me like I was a long-lost daughter. The smell of fresh-baked apple pie blows into my face. Who'd be baking an apple pie in Foggy Bottom? In a low whispery voice that raises the hairs along the back of my neck, for it's the same Voice that caused me to set fire to a tub mill, someone hidden by mist starts in singing a lullaby to me:

Hush, little baby, don't say a word,
Mama's gonna buy you a mockingbird.

26

Over the past few weeks, I've learned some important things. The first is not to trust in a voice that comes out of the Foggy Bottom mist! That trust could land me in the Francis Spittle Home for Wayward Girls! The second is—love exists—it can help you face most anything. Putting my hand on the golden locket which awakened love in me, I face the mist that's acting like a momma and making me long to be with one and I say aloud them three magic words Miss Hope taught me:

Amor Vincit Omnia!

The Voice hisses like hog grease hitting a hot frying pan and them misty arms let me go. The mist backs off, taking with it the apple-pie smell and leaving me with the stench of mud and rotted leaves. I scream at that fool mist and whoever's hidden in it: "You'd better go on and leave me alone or next time, I'll love-charm you into extinction!"

The mist goes pop like a pig bladder that's been stuck

and then, a thick silent fog creeps in, settling around me so now I don't see nothing. Nothing at all. I feel more alone than I have in my entire life. I wish I had them Darnells with me. I call out, "Eatmore Beans, where are you?"

"I'm coming!" he mutters from somewhere I can't see. At last, he trots out of the deep fog and down the creek bank to where I'm standing. He looks up at me and says, "Hoot! Look at you—wet and muddy as a bog! You're not at all what the lad's expecting."

"Then why are you taking me to him?" I shout at the cat. I ain't feeling so good right now.

"I'm taking you because my little laddie with the white hair, my Baby Earl, asked me to and so I will," he shouts back, which I reckon is as fair an answer as any. He says, "Follow me and keep to the road. If you stray off it, you'll end up in the heart of Foggy Bottom and you'll never come out of it again!"

He scuttles away so fast, I can't see him for the fog, although I do hear him muttering, "The best-laid plans of cats and men gang aft a-gley," whatever that means.

"Eatmore Beans! I can't see you!" I cry out.

He lights up his tail for me. Being a gray tabby cat, he has a ringed tail and by magic he's lit up the paler rings for me to follow. I ain't never seen nothing like this. The murky edge of Foggy Bottom is one peculiar place where I reckon anything can happen and it will.

I run after Eatmore's five bobbing rings of light—up the creek bank and onto Piney Gap Road. Beneath my feet, I feel the hard outline of hoofprints—no doubt left by them North Carolina bushwhackers, coming up from Gobbler's Glen to attack our cove. They ain't attacked our cove in three years, but still, I feel their hoofprints. If I had me the time, I'd rub out each and every one of them prints. No part of any Rebel bushwhacker belongs in Mary's Cove and it never will!

I continue to hear Tucker Creek over to my right, which is reassuring to me because it lets me know in which direction Mary's Cove lies as I trot after Eatmore Beans through a silent fog grown thick as pork loin gravy. If worst comes to worst, and I get lost in the fog, I can always head toward the creek.

Will this road that skirts the dangerous border between my world and Foggy Bottom lead me to Goodlow? I trust it will. I trust each step I take brings me closer to the boy I love. I'll save him. I'll bring him home. Why, that should be bail enough to even free my grandpa. The thought of all this makes my heartbeat quicken. The road turns steep and rocky. Scrub oak and dog-hobble on either side try to crowd me off it. I plow on through, branches grabbing at my dress and at my violet-smelling hair.

Ahead of me, the Swamp Cat stops so fast, I almost bump into him. He whispers, "Listen, lassie, do you hear?"

I don't hear nothing but my heart.

"The bogies, lass; I hear bogies marching. The swamp tree must have sounded the alarum. If the bogies find us, they'll stop our getting to Goodlow and here we are, so close to him!" Flattening himself, Eatmore Beans scurries off to the right of the road and into a patch of dog-hobble.

"Eatmore Beans! I can't step off the road!" I scream.

"You can if it's on the creek side," he calls back.

"Well, how was I to know that?" Can I trust the Swamp Cat? Baby Earl would say I could. I scramble into the dog-hobble after the cat. I crawl through the thicket—fighting off the shrubby branches trying to tear at my hair and skirt. I ain't never met one of them Warrior Bogies face-to-face, but Buffer has. He says them bogies ain't got no legs, which does make me wonder how they march. I follow Eatmore Beans out of the dog-hobble and up onto a rocky rise and I don't have to wonder how them bogies march no more.

Them stump-like bogies hop like a spring. How do I know this? Because a catfish black bogie about the size of Baby Earl springs through thick gray fog, brandishing its stinging tentacle and shrieking at me, "Gnat-a-bunga!"

27

I'm so startled by the bogie shrieking my name with a bunga, I fall backward onto my bottom, which is a good thing because it causes the bogie's stinging tentacle to miss me by a whisper. Here I trusted Eatmore Beans and he led me into a bogie trap! Whipping back its tentacle to try and strike at me again, the bogie springs at me, its hole of a mouth wide open—its tiny pointed teeth ready to tear at my flesh. I throw up my arms to defend myself and do you know who sails through the foggy air to rescue me? The same cat I just thought had betrayed me—Eatmore Beans!

Shouting at me, "Bad poem, lassie!" that brave cat, his lit tail growed real big, attacks the bogie five times his size. He grabs hold of the bogie's stinging tentacle with his front paws and his teeth. The bogie lifts Eatmore Beans into the air; he clings to the swaying tentacle. The bogie must be stinging Eatmore Beans real bad—the cat's gray tabby hair stands up on end.

I struggle to my feet while trying to come up with a bad poem to defeat the bogie, but the rhyming words won't come. They just won't come! The bogie whips his tentacle around Eatmore Beans; that bogie's gonna squeeze the Swamp Cat to death! I grab up what I think is a stick to hit that evil bogie on its catfish head. The stick writhes in my hand. It ain't no stick; it's a stout-bodied hog-nosed snake!

I fling the snake at the bogie. The snake lands on the bogie's head; that snake goes belly-up like it was kilt dead. That's when the bad poem comes to me and it don't have nothing to do with the snake:

> Gnat-a-bunga, evil bogie!
> Gnat-a-bunga, howdy-do!
> You ain't nothing but a catfish stump
> Unfit for poor-boy stew!
> Gnat Stokes and Eatmore Beans—
> We'll make fishbait out of you.

I tell you, there ain't nothing like the power of a bad poem. My poem stuns the bogie! All of a sudden-like, it can't seem to move. I yell at it, "Let go of Eatmore Beans!" The bogie does, which does surprise me. It makes me think I'm the bogie's queen and that he's in my power.

The noble cat tumbles to the ground. Quicker than you can say, "Queen Gnat," the hog-nosed snake, not kilt at all but only playing at it, slithers off into the dog-hobble. I yell at the stunned bogie, "Be gone!" That bogie melts into a black pool, which disappears into the dirt.

As for Eatmore Beans? The brave Swamp Cat lies where he fell.

"Eatmore Beans, be healed and rise!" I say in the same bossy tone I used with the bogie.

It don't work.

"Eatmore Beans? Are you all right?" I lay down so I can look into his big gold eyes. They look real tired to me. He tries to raise his head, but it must be too heavy for him, because he can't. Swallowing to hold back my tears, I stroke his gray tabby coat. I thought he'd betrayed me. He breathes real shallow-like as all the magic light slowly drains out of his ringed tail—which has come down to its normal size. Thick fog wraps itself around us so that all I can see is the cat in front of me. I say, "Eatmore Beans, we kilt the bogie!

"Eatmore Beans, don't die."

"Eatmore Beans loves the little white-haired laddie," he whispers.

"I know you do." Sobbing, I say, "I saw how you two slept; I couldn't tell where you ended and Baby Earl began."

"He's my laddie," Eatmore gasps.

"I'll get you back to him, I promise!"

"You must save Goodlow first," he says.

"Goodlow must be someone real special for you to say that." I stroke Eatmore's head.

"Aye, lassie. He tried to name me. It took a bonnie little lad to name me." I feel a shudder pass through Eatmore Beans.

"He must be in awful pain," a voice at my back says.

I freeze. It's the Voice I heard earlier. It whispers in my ear, *"Follow the Jack-O'-Lantern Trail. It'll lead you to a momma who'll make the cat feel fine and sassy."*

"What momma? What Jack-O'-Lantern Trail?" I know I shouldn't be talking to a Voice. But I'm on my own with a dying cat I don't have no power to save.

"Turn around," the Voice says.

Beyond the swirls of mist the Voice seems to be hiding in, a trail has appeared. Lit green by jack-o'-lantern mushrooms sprouting from tree stumps like warts on a witch's nose, the trail heads downhill into the heart of Foggy Bottom, where I ain't supposed to go for fear I'll never come back out. I'd be lying if I told you I didn't want to take that trail, for I see, standing at the end of it, the kind of cozy firelit cabin in which a momma bakes apple pies for her young 'uns and tends to ailing Swamp Cats.

"Can I trust a Voice that caused me to burn down a tub mill?" I ask it.

"I like your poetry," it whispers.

"Do you like me?" I say.

"You're my daughter," it says.

"I ain't no daughter of a Voice that can't admit to liking me!" I go to say my Latin love charm and no sooner do I get the first word out—*"Amor"*—than the Voice hisses and the swirls of mist it seems to come from disappear. But the Jack-O'-Lantern Trail and that little cabin don't.

I want Granny with me. I want her, Grandpa Stokes and them Darnells, too. I'm feeling scairt and lonely. I turn to Eatmore Beans. The fog's grown real thick around him since we don't have his glowing tail rings to light it up no more.

"Eatmore Beans?" I whisper into one of the cat's little turned-down ears. "A Foggy Bottom Voice has lit up a Jack-O'-Lantern Trail for us to follow and I'm wondering—"

"That Voice belongs to Zelda!" Eatmore gasps.

Zelda's saying she's my momma?

"Don't take the trail!" Eatmore gasps.

"Well then, Eatmore Beans, what am I supposed to do? I ain't got your lit tail to help me see my way to Goodlow." I want to be back in Mary's Cove with the folks I know who've named and taken care of me.

Zelda's saying she's my momma.

"We're so close to him." Eatmore shivers so hard, his teeth chatter. I pick him up and hold him close. If I'm Zelda's daughter, how come I ain't got no magic power?

If I had power, I'd heal this cat. After a little, Eatmore's shivering does stop. Looking up at me, he says, "You're a bonnier lass than I first thought. Sing a love song for the lad. It might break the spell that chains him to his prison cell and draw him out here to you."

"I ain't known for singing love songs," I say.

"If you sing from your heart, it won't matter," Eatmore says and then, as if the pain's just too much for him, he shuts his eyes tight. "Sing your own special love song."

"Eatmore Beans? I ain't got a love song!" I wail.

28

When a hurt Swamp Cat asks you to sing your special love song, you got to sing something. The song I finally settle on ain't exactly mine; it's a favorite of everyone in Mary's Cove—"Sourwood Mountain." Before the war, my pappy would fiddle the tune to "Sourwood Mountain" at barn dances. He'd stroke, tease and whang his fiddle until even DeWitt Lawson couldn't stand still. I'd keep time with my clackers. Pappy, chinning his fiddle, would smile over at me. I felt real proud. I recollect Goodlow and Penelope singing the song in harmony. Folks' feet would fly:

> Chickens a-crowin' on Sourwood Mountain
> Hey-ho, dee-iddle-um-day.
> Call up your dogs and let's go a-huntin',
> Hey-ho, dee-iddle-um-day.

It ain't exactly a love song neither. But folks in Mary's Cove do love it. I sing out into the fog all eight verses I know of the song while holding Eatmore Beans in my arms to keep us both warm. The fog's grown real dark and chilly and Eatmore's done passed out.

When Goodlow don't appear on the first go-round of the song, I sing it a second time. And then a third. I make sure to keep the Jack-O'-Lantern Trail at my back so I won't see a momma's cozy firelit cabin. If I take the trail that leads to it, I might never come back out. If I don't come out, who'll save Goodlow Pryce? To say nothing of Grandpa Stokes, suffocating from dander in DeWitt Lawson's jail cell. Who'll read *Ten Nights in a Bar-Room* to them Darnells? And listen to Granny Hart's sermons? Who'll borrow *Little Women* from Miss Hope?

Here I'm singing a love song for Goodlow and it's bringing all them Mary's Cove folk to mind. I love them folk. They mean more to me than any old Swamp Queen.

I sing out:

> My true love's a brown-eyed daisy,
> Hey-ho, dee-iddle-um-day.
> If I don't get him, I'll go crazy,
> Hey-ho, dee-iddle-um-day.

And something out there in the fog behind me goes *boogety, boogety*. I stop my love singing and huddle myself around Eatmore Beans for safekeeping—his and mine. Because there ain't but one creature I know who goes *boogety, boogety*—Zelda's terrifying Foggy Bottom Swamp Guard—the Boogety Bear.

From the boogety sounds that bear continues to make, I can tell it's headed my way. If Jib were here, she'd be shrieking at me, "Cover your innards! Watch your backside! Run!"

But with the thick fog, I can't see to run. The fog around me turns an eerie shade of green. Is it from the Swamp Bear's glowing coat? I ain't never seen that coat because Grandpa always sat on me when them Swampers paraded through Mary's Cove. I wish I was back home with Grandpa sitting on me right now.

I don't like hiding in the deep fog with something in it stalking me.

"Boogety, boogety," something now says at my back.

"Boogety, boogety," I say, and turn to bravely face whatever fate awaits me.

29

That fate ain't what I expect—a huge clawed and vicious creature attacking me and tearing me to shreds. The Boogety Bear, glowing gray-green all over with what looks like fox fire, stands upright on his hairy hind legs and, instead of attacking, he peers down his long bear nose at me. He's wearing a thick collar around his furry neck, with a broken chain dangling from it. He ain't got normal bear paws but pale green and human-looking hands and feet. The expression in his small dark eyes appears human-like as well. After taking a good long look at me with the cat, he roars as if the word's been ripped out of his heart—"NOOOOOOOOOO!" Then he turns and he runs away from me—his huge shaggy coat lighting up the fog.

Is he part human?

He's the only light in this here fog.

Holding on to Eatmore Beans, I run after the bear, now heading up Piney Gap.

"Why'd you roar 'No' at me?" I call out to the bear.

He don't answer. Dropping on all fours, he climbs

through a heap of windfall fallen across the road. Rising on his hind legs once more, he continues up the road in the direction Eatmore Beans and I had been taking before being waylaid by the Warrior Bogie.

I hear the bear saying to himself, "Boogety, boogety," and then, I see him shrug. It's like he's saying to himself something awful, but it's true and he might as well accept it with a shrug and keep on going. Like if I should say to myself, "I think I have an evil Swamp Queen for a momma."

I want to touch him in the center of his shrug. Right there in the glowing center of that hump below the collar on his neck. I want to touch him there even though Wanda would say to me, "Gnat! Touching a Swamp Bear ain't smart!"

And Jib would say, "He'll turn around and kill you."

"He ain't got no claws to kill me," I'd tell Jib.

"He's still got his sharp teeth," she'd answer.

I ain't scairt of teeth! I want to touch his hump. I want to do it more than I've wanted to do anything short of saving Goodlow Pryce. Something now sings inside my head: Do it, do it, do it!

Running through fog that, with darkness coming, has turned the color of burnt pork gravy, I draw ever closer to the glowing bear. Heart pounding, I finally reach out and touch the Boogety Bear on that furry shoulder hump that draws me like a bee to pollen.

Soon as I do, the bear stops dead like he's been shot. He throws up his hairy hands and shakes all over. The hump I touched starts splitting open. From there, his entire back splits open like the skin on a ripe tomato and the bear falls on his face because he ain't got no firm back now to hold him up.

Oh no! My touch has kilt the Swamp Bear!

30

Hugging Eatmore Beans, I draw close to get a look at the bear I kilt with my one hand and discover something about the bear ain't dead. Something's going on inside his body. Why, the Boogety Bear's got a grown boy inside his body! A live boy dressed all in black! He climbs out of that glowing bear's body, lying open on the ground like a pair of empty overalls waiting to be put back on, and he stumbles to large, splayed feet.

There ain't but one boy I know who has feet like these—Goodlow Pryce. He don't seem to have a single bite mark on him, so I reckon the Boogety Bear didn't chew him up and swallow him. I reckon Goodlow Pryce *was* the Boogety Bear. Zelda must have done this to him, turned a precious boy into a huge and frightening guard bear.

I freed Goodlow with my touch.

He's got a dazed-like expression in his eyes which reminds me of Wanda, when she's been snoring deeply and I just woke her up to make her stop. I give Goodlow a moment to recollect who he is and the song I sung that brought him out from where Zelda had done chained him up. The glow from his discarded bear body lights the fog around us to a pale green and through it I see Goodlow's precious eyes—dark and with a hint of gold in them.

Soon as them eyes settle on me with Eatmore Beans, that sweet boy groans and slumps to the ground where he sits and rocks, covering his face with his hands. He don't look real pleased to see me. I settle myself alongside him. *Goodlow's here.* He appears taller than I am and real thin. I love his long dark hair, curly and wild.

I say real soft-like to him, "Howdy."

"Boogety, boogety," he says.

"I don't understand that kind of talk," I say.

He clears his throat. He swallows. Still rocking, he says to the ruffles on his black shirt, "I'm wondering what happened to the little Swamp Cat."

"A Warrior Bogie stung Eatmore Beans," I say.

"Someone named the cat?" Goodlow's rocking slows.

"Baby Earl named him," I say.

"Is Baby Earl a . . . a mortal boy?" he says.

"He's a mortal boy with white hair," I say.

Goodlow stops rocking altogether. He removes his hands from his face and sweeps his wild dark hair back from his bold and noble-looking forehead. Without looking at me, he says, "Can I look at the cat?"

"Why, sure you can." I go to hand him Eatmore

Beans and he says, "No. While I look at the cat, you need to keep a hold of him." So I do and Goodlow puts his arms around me, and then, he presses his ear to my chest, not the cat's! I ain't never saw no one examine a hurt creature this way, but I can tell you this. It don't bother me none. I love the warmth of being held in Goodlow's arms. I love his wild hair and the singular quality of his curls, each seeming to go its own way with extenuating passion. One of them curls touches my chin and my heart starts beating loud as a tom-tom.

Goodlow moves on to press his ear against Eatmore Beans. After several moments, Goodlow says, "The cat has a mortal heartbeat."

"Are you sure it's the cat's?" It could be mine. My heart is working double time.

"I know a heartbeat when I hear one," Goodlow says. "Your Baby Earl rightly named the cat and now he has a heart! It's the first step in turning a swamp creature into a mortal one. The changing ain't easy, but it can be done.

"I tried to name the cat myself," he says. "I tried and I tried."

"I tried to name him, too," I say.

"That makes us two beans in a pod," Goodlow says.

"I reckon it does." *Two beans in a pod.*

"I heard your heartbeat. You ain't Swamp. You're mortal like me." Goodlow raises his head from Eatmore's side. Goodlow's brown eyes with all them gold flecks in them rest on mine. I love his eyes. I love his mouth, now breaking forth into a crooked smile. He says, "Keep the Swamp Cat against your strong heart. Keep him there until you turn him over to the boy who named him. It's that boy he belongs with and who'll save him for the long run. Once he's in the boy's arms, I reckon the Swamp Cat will complete his entire transformation to a mortal one. He'll purr."

"Far as I know, Eatmore Beans ain't never purred." I can't take my eyes off Goodlow's.

"Swamp Cats don't purr. But mortal ones do." He runs a warm hand down my cheek and I feel like purring. He whispers, "Your mortal skin's so soft and warm. I ain't touched mortal skin in almost seven years."

"You can touch mine all you want," I say.

"Do you know who I am?" He runs his warm hand down my throat.

"You're Goodlow Pryce." I find myself talking the way he does—low and soft-like. "You're from Mary's Cove. You was kidnapped by the Swamp Queen, seven years ago tomorrow, which is All Hallows' Eve. You're in trouble and I have come to save you."

"Can I trust you?" Goodlow asks.

"Course you can," I say as his hand comes to a rest on my collarbone, where the necklace disappears beneath the edge of my pretty flowered dress. He lifts the necklace and pulls out the enchanted locket with the name *Penelope* on it.

I wish he hadn't found the locket, for as soon as he touches it, why . . . it . . . it feels like a love spell's been broken. Not on my part, but on Goodlow's. He drops the locket, draws his warmth away from me and says in a harsh voice, "What are you doing with this locket! You ain't Penelope!"

"No I ain't. I'm Gnat Stokes. Eatmore Beans flew out of the air and I caught him. He had that there locket hanging from his mouth. I took it away from him and I put it on." This is all the truth.

"And you kept it for yourself," he says.

"Yes I did." I ain't lying to a boy I want loving me.

"You're Gnat Stokes from Mary's Cove," he says.

"Yes I am." *He knows me. At least he knows me.*

"Gnat—a two-winged pesky critter sort of like a mosquito and when she bites, she makes you itch." He gives me his crooked grin.

"That's right." I do love my name; it fits me.

"I remember your naming ceremony," Goodlow says. He don't look so angry now that he understands and knows me.

"I came upon your pappy back here in July," he says.

"You did?" What was my no-good pappy doing here?

"He'd been hoofing it up Piney Gap—on his way to Gobbler's Glen after trying to hook up with you," Goodlow goes on. "I ain't never seen a man so sorry-looking. He misses you, Gnat. He stopped awhile to play his fiddle—not far from here.

"His fiddling drew me out the same way your singing did. He wasn't afraid of me—even though he saw me as a bear! He talked to me like I was human. He talked and he talked. He told me, given your gnat-like nature that likes to poke into forbidden places, no doubt I'd be seeing you sooner or later and here you are.

"Gnat, can I trust you to do a favor for me?" Goodlow says.

"Course you can." I'd do anything for this boy. Even listening to him talk about my pappy like he was a good man—which he ain't!

Goodlow says, "Will you take Penelope Drinkwater a message from me?"

31

The last person I want to take a message to from Goodlow is Penelope. She thinks he's her sweetheart. I want him to be mine, but I don't dare tell him this. I just nod and say, "I reckon I can do it."

And he draws close to me once more. He whispers to me like it's the most important thing in the world and he don't want no one but me alone to hear, "Tell Penelope to be at the Hallelujah Pond tomorrow night—All Hallows' Eve—by midnight. Tell her to bring that green cloak of hers."

"The pond. All Hallows' Eve. Midnight. A green cloak," I whisper up at him. I wonder where all this is leading and where I could find me a cloak like that.

"She should hide herself until she sees me come."

"Will you be a Swamp Bear?"

"I'll be myself," he says.

"Well, I know some changing sheds Penelope can hide behind until she sees you." I could easily hide behind them sheds myself. "You know the sheds I mean? It's where folks changed into their white gowns before being baptized in the Hallelujah Pond. I ain't never been inside them sheds," I allow. "My pappy done run off Preacher John before I got my chance to be baptized."

"Zelda kidnapped me before I got mine," Goodlow says.

"That truly makes us *two beans in a pod*." It gives me pleasure to repeat the same words Goodlow said earlier. He covers my one free hand with his, while my other holds on to Eatmore Beans, still breathing.

I love this boy.

"Tell Penelope, at midnight, Zelda and her Swampers will parade on by the pond on their way to Devil's Notch," he whispers real urgent-like. Well, no wonder. Time's growing short. "Penelope should let the first two groups of Swampers go on by. She shouldn't look too close at them; they'll scare her. I'll be in the third group. I'll be riding a pure white mule."

"A pure white mule," I whisper. He still covers my hand with his. Does he love my mortal touch?

I love his.

"Once she sees me, Penelope should burst forth from hiding," he whispers. "With one hand, she's to grab the white mule by the bridle to make him stop. With the other, she's to grab my left hand and pull me off the mule."

As he says this, I slip my thumb over his thumb,

turn my hand slightly and now I'm holding on to his hand as much as he's holding on to mine.

I want to be the one to save this boy.

"Soon as Penelope pulls me to the ground, Zelda will try to scare her into letting go of me," he says. "Zelda will shriek and carry on. Tell my sweet gal, 'Don't be afraid of Zelda. Hold fast to your Goodlow.' And then the Swamp Queen will work her fearful magic on me and there ain't nothing I can do about it. She'll change me from one terrifying creature into another.

"Tell Penelope to hold on to me. She should hold on to me no matter how terrifying I become, for she is my own true love and I would never hurt her. I will go through four transformations. The fourth and final one will be the worst, for Zelda will turn me into a hot bar of burning iron—too hot for even my Penelope to handle. That's when she should throw me into the holy water of the Hallelujah Pond—in the deep, deep center of it.

"Whatever comes out of the water, Penelope should cover with that green cloak of hers and we shall see what we shall see."

"That pond's grown real murky," I say.

"The center's still clear," he says.

"Do you know how to swim?" I say.

"I know how to float," he says.

"How you gonna float if you're a bar of iron?" I say.

"I don't know," he says.

I don't like the sound of this. If Penelope lets go of Goodlow—which I'm sure she will—he'll drown.

It should be me at the pond. I'd never let him go. I don't care if he burned me to a crisp. Still holding on to Goodlow's hand, I say, "Goodlow. Penelope ain't the gal to do this for you—I am."

32

nat," Goodlow says. I love the way he breathes my name. It makes it sound as if it's the most natural and beautiful name in the world, which it is. "I'm real grateful for what you're offering to do for me. I ain't seen such heartfelt generosity in almost seven years. Except from the Swamp Cat who tried to take Penelope a message from me. But . . ." He stops to clear his throat. He even does this in a beautiful way. "But you got to understand. I can only be saved by the gal who truly, truly loves me."

"I love you," I say. Can't he see this? Can't he feel the kind of love I'm feeling? It makes me feel real warm inside.

He looks into my eyes and says soft and gentle-like, "You ain't in love with me. You're in love with love. On account of that love-enchanted locket you have on. When I made it, I poured into it all my love for Penelope."

"The love I'm feeling is my own true love for you." I feel this is the most honest and true thing I've said all day. I love his hair, his noble forehead, his eyes, his crooked smile, his hand in mine . . .

He shakes his head. He don't believe me. He says, "If my own true love Penelope ain't at the pond to save me, Zelda will take me on up to Devil's Notch and sacrifice me to the devil himself."

"No!" I don't believe it! This is something Jib would think up—the worst of the worst!

"It's true, Gnat." Goodlow squeezes my hand. He needs someone to hold on to even now. Why can't it always be me? I think my heart is breaking. He says, "Every seven years, Zelda sacrifices a mortal like me to pay the devil for her own immortality—which means she don't ever die. Nor have a loving heart like yours that cares for someone other than her own self."

"Zelda don't have a heart?" I say.

"No she don't. And she don't ever want one. She's told me if she don't give me over to the devil, she may as well die here and now. For he'll turn her into a mortal woman—thirty-seven years old, with rheumatism setting in, red hair starting to turn gray and a heart that can break."

A heart like mine.

I want her to feel the pain I feel. Goodlow loves Penelope—not me.

"I'll take Penelope your message," I say.

"You will?" he says.

"I will."

"I got something special to help light your way back to Penelope through all the fog," Goodlow says. "It's something your pappy asked me to pass on to you. It's from your momma. Meant for you on your twelfth birthday."

Goodlow reaches inside his bear body and he brings out from it that old sow's ear of a birthday present Pappy tried to pawn off on me this past July. Only now, in the dark fog with Goodlow, something inside that ear is causing it to glow a pretty shade of lady slipper green.

33

Itake the glowing ear from Goodlow; the ear fits easily into the palm of my right hand—just like it belongs there. This ear came in my baby basket. Should I open it up? Goodlow must sense my hesitation, for he says, "Your pappy said whatever's inside the ear is your birthright. It's meant for you and no one else. He thinks it's something magical. But he couldn't get the ear open to find out."

"It's just like Pappy to try and open something meant for me." That no-good bushwhacker.

"He wanted to make sure there wasn't something in it that would harm you. He cares for you, Gnat. He said he wants to put the war behind him and come to have a good long visit with you. He misses your keeping time to his fiddling. Without you on the clackers, he can't get his rhythms right."

"I reckon music is a tie that binds us." It sure ain't politics. I hunker over Eatmore Beans, cradling him between my chest and lap so I can free both hands to open up the glowing sow's ear, which, if nothing else, can help me find my way home through the fog. As I do, I notice something peculiar about the Swamp Cat. Eatmore Beans is making music of his own. He's snoring. He wasn't snoring earlier, but he is now.

Is this the ear's doing? With trembling hands, I untie the horse tail hair holding it together. The sow's ear unfolds easily and of its own accord. Inside is something so surprising, it clean takes my breath away. It's a gold ring with a glowing stone in it—the green color of a lady slipper's leaves. Inside the bright and glowing stone, an eye looks out at me. It looks like a gentle loving momma's eye.

Why, it's the prettiest ring I ever did see. I slip it onto the fourth finger of my right hand and I feel a surge of power that makes all the hairs on my arms stand up on end. In my arms, Eatmore stirs. He opens his eyes.

"Lord have mercy. That's a magic ring." Goodlow looks from the ring to the now wide-awake cat. Goodlow says, "There ain't but one other person I know who has a magic ring like that one you have on, only the eye in hers ain't sweet but evil looking."

"You're not talking about Zelda?" I say.

"Do you know what this means?" he says.

"That I'm the Swamp Queen's daughter." I figured as much.

"I'd better get back to my cave." Goodlow scrambles to his feet.

He's scairt of me on account of who my momma is. He goes to climb into his bear body, but before he can, I grab his pants leg with my ringed hand and I say, "Stop."

He does and I scramble to my feet. I grab hold of his hand, look up at him and I say, "Now you listen to me. I ain't my momma. I ain't my pappy. I'm Gnat and I got me a heart so full of love for you, I reckon it's what's caused this here ring to glow so sweet.

"I'd do anything for you," I say.

Goodlow don't look at me. He doesn't believe me!

"Tell you what." I take a deep breath. I need air for what I'm gonna say next. "The whole time you was giving me the message for Penelope I was thinking I wouldn't take it to her because I wanted to be the one to save you. But I see now that that ain't gonna work. I'll take Penelope your message, Goodlow." I can't believe I said this. "I'll even escort that poor shortsighted gal to the Hallelujah Pond for you."

Goodlow still don't look like he believes me.

"I swear this, Goodlow. I swear it all upon my heart." *Please believe me.*

Goodlow's eyes now come to rest on mine. He says, "Gnat, I trust your heart." And then, as if to seal his trust, this precious boy takes my face into his hands and he kisses me so soft and full upon my willing mouth, I'm like to swoon.

34

Time must travel different on the murky edge of Foggy Bottom. While it feels like I only passed a few hours there, I reckon I spent the entire night and part of the next day. For when I finally enter Mary's Cove after hotfooting it down Piney Gap with my ring lighting the way, I find I can step on the head of my shadow, which means it's noon or close to it. Grandpa's trial is set for noon today at the First Baptist Church. Wish I had Goodlow to go there with me.

If I had Goodlow with me, folks would be so happy, they'd free Grandpa on the spot.

Goodlow kissed me.

I feel his kiss of trust upon my mouth as I hotfoot it away from Tucker Creek with Eatmore Beans wide-awake in my arms and my green ring glowing. It lit my way home and no momma tried to lure me into Foggy Bottom. I reckon she's saving all her magic power for tonight's showdown at the Hallelujah Pond! All Hallows' Eve is almost here.

Eatmore now says to me, *Hurry. Get me to my lad-*

die. I want to purr in my little laddie's arms. Only Eatmore's mouth don't move like it did before that Warrior Bogie stung him. Instead, I hear him talking to me in my head. He's been word-thoughting me like this ever since my ring done woke him up. He told me then, *Gnat Stokes, you have a ring of healing power.*

I reckon I do and look who passed it down to me—the Swamp Queen! Once she's mortal (she better become mortal, because if she don't, Goodlow becomes the devil's own and I can't bear the thought of that), maybe I'll heal her of her rheumatism. But that's only if I want to.

Since the Darnells' cabin is on my way to the church, I head to the cabin first. It feels good to be out of the fog and running through sunlight where I can see leaves all turned their pretty fall shades and corn stubble, golden in the fields, and a lone hawk soaring through a clear blue sky.

I follow a short path through the woods and over to the back side of the Darnells' cabin so that I can reunite Eatmore Beans with Baby Earl. There ain't the customary noises issuing forth from the cabin—pots banging and the occasional shriek—"Studs! You leave Baby Earl alone!" On the sagging back porch, there is a plank shelf nailed between two posts where the Darnells do their washing-up when something cataclysmic warrants it. On the plank is a basin filled with dirty water. Nearby, wet towels are draped over the porch rail. I call around for Baby Earl. No one comes running.

"I reckon they're all at the church for Grandpa's trial," I tell Eatmore Beans.

Get us to the church! Eatmore word-thoughts me.

I light out for the First Baptist Church quicker than a hornet bent on stinging a sow's behind. I ain't seen the insides of that church but a few times and each time I did, I carried on so loud, Grandpa had to haul me out. But I was little and now I'm all growed up.

I don't slow until I reach the church's wagon lot with mules and horses drowsing at their hitching posts. I edge on past them toward the church that's in sore need of repair—its white paint's peeling and two windows have been shot out. The mules mostly just yawn at me, but several horses roll their eyes and DeWitt Lawson's silly chestnut mare throws back her head so hard, she breaks her tether and trots off.

I sidle by Vera May Clauser's buckboard, its top board covered with upside-down horseshoes to ward off Swamp Witches. I head toward the two closed church doors—one marked Men, the other, Women.

DeWitt Lawson's voice comes from the other side of them two church doors. He's castigating Grandpa from the pulpit!

"Nathaniel Stokes don't deserve any of our heartfelt leniency," that DeWitt's saying at the top of his raspy voice. "He broke our law against having moonshine. Not only that, he got boastful about it—pouring it over the ground! Now all our innocent and precious children can smell it. Why, they could become intoxicated! Worse still and compounding our injury is that this low-down whiskey-drinker and conniver is a thief! Upon investigating his cabin, I found inside it my own book—*Ten Nights in a Bar-Room and I Was There*!"

Grandpa didn't steal that book, I did.

I slowly open the door in front of me and peer inside the dimly lit church as DeWitt is saying, "Moreover, he must have done something terrible to Gnat. That granddaughter of his, who burned down our one tub mill and caused Vera May's cow to give bubble milk for three days straight, has plumb disappeared."

"I ain't disappeared!" I say.

Everyone turns to gape at me. It looks like everyone in Mary's Cove has come to witness Grandpa's trial. I got the men of Mary's Cove seated to my right. I got the women seated to my left, including Granny Hart and Miss Hope with Penelope seated between them. Taking a deep breath, I step through the open door and the glowing ring I have on causes the dark insides of a church that ain't been used for religious purposes in almost seven years to turn green.

I stop. My feet don't seem to want to move forward no more. I ain't sure why. Is it because I'm part Swamp?

Will marching into church make me shrivel up and die? Down the green aisle in front of me stands Baby Earl in clean overalls. That sweet boy stands on the Castigation Spot alongside my grandpa, which is where I should be. Baby Earl holds on to Grandpa's one hand. Loyal Wanda, with stalwart Jib alongside her, holds on to Grandpa's other. Grandpa don't look so good, but no wonder. He spent the entire night in DeWitt's jail cell!

Behind Grandpa towers DeWitt Lawson himself and I can smell him clear down the church aisle. He smells like a dead dog in the rain. Dander from his scraggly brown hair covers the shoulders of his shiny black suit. The hatchet-faced deacon shouts for all to hear—"Heaven protect us! Gnat's got on a ring just like the Swamp Queen's!"

"Gnat's a Swamp Witch!" Vera May shrieks.

"I may be part Swamp, but I ain't no witch," I shout above the hubbub broken out around me. Taking a deep breath, I force my feet to move, one foot in front of the other. I hold my head high. "No witch could enter this here church. It would shrivel her to death." I ain't shriveling—praise be. "I'm Gnat," I say. "Named so by each and every one of you. Because of you, I got me a heart. A heart that has learned to love in more ways than you can count." I come to a stop in front of Grandpa Stokes and them Darnells. My glowing ring turns all their faces green.

"Howdy, Gnat," them Darnells say—all three.

Grandpa don't say nothing.

"Howdy-do," I say to them Darnells. "I'm real sorry I couldn't wait for you yesterday. The cat took off on me." I feel Grandpa's eyes taking me in as I hand over Eatmore Beans to Baby Earl. "This is one courageous cat," I tell Baby Earl. "He fought a Warrior Bogie on my behalf and almost died. I'm gonna miss his body against my heart and his voice inside my head, but he belongs to you. He missed you, Baby Earl."

Baby Earl hugs Eatmore Beans.

The cat, now being held against the heart of the little boy who loves him and who will save him for the long run, breaks down and purrs.

I hear behind me folks getting to their feet. Folks are muttering, "She's a Swamp Witch."

"My Gnat ain't no Swamp Witch!" Grandpa shouts at them. I love my grandpa. Turning to me, he says, "By God, Gnat, where have you been?" He runs his hand down my cheek and then, my arm, as if he can't believe I'm truly here. *Grandpa loves me.*

"I've been out looking for Goodlow Pryce," I say.

Folks stop muttering at the sound of Goodlow's name.

There's an awed hush that could quiet a stampeding mule. DeWitt Lawson's jaw drops wide open.

"Did you find him?" Grandpa whispers.

"Yes, Grandpa, I did," I say out loud for all to hear. "And if Penelope Drinkwater don't meet him at the Hallelujah Pond by midnight, tonight, the Swamp Queen will sacrifice that sweet boy to the devil!"

"My sweetheart? My Goodlow?" Penelope rises to her feet with Granny Hart and Miss Hope alongside her.

And I can't believe what I'm seeing! Penelope, the gal who's supposed to save Goodlow by grabbing his mule, pulling him off it and then holding on to him with her two strong arms while my momma puts him through her fearful transformations, has her right arm in a sling!

35

Even the best and most thought-out plans can be messed up by the dark. Last night, in the dark, Penelope tripped over her own washing log and she fell, landing the wrong way. She broke her right arm and bruised her right leg real bad. She's telling me all about it now in Preacher John's old consult room. Miss Hope and Granny hauled Penelope and me in here for a heart-to-heart concerning Goodlow after Granny shouted at DeWitt Lawson and everyone else, "Put the trial on hold! We need to be alone to talk to Gnat. This is a matter of true love, not law."

"I'd been out sleepwalking," Penelope is confiding in me like I was her best friend. She's got tears in her eyes, which makes me feel real sorry for her. "I dreamt I was going after Goodlow. He called to me from across the creek, 'Follow Gnat. Gnat knows the way to me.' I turned to find you, Gnat. And that's when I tripped."

"Gnat will reunite you with your boy," Granny tells Penelope while glaring at me.

"Yes, Granny, I will," I say as she settles Penelope into Preacher John's old cane chair. Miss Hope comforts Penelope by patting her on the shoulder. I want Miss Hope to comfort me. I need me a teacher more than ever.

"We got us a problem," I say. "Goodlow needs a gal with two strong arms to save him." I go on to explain the entire situation regarding the saving of Goodlow, including the fact that it's my own momma who'll be putting him through his fearful transformations while the gal who truly loves him holds on and doesn't let him go. It's my own momma who'll sacrifice him to the devil so that she won't become a mortal woman, thirty-seven years old with the rheumatism setting in and a heart that can break.

My own momma—the Swamp Queen.

As I talk, my birthright ring glows, turning the room a soft shade of green. The ring's eye gazes sweetly up at me.

"That's one powerful ring," Granny says when I've done talking. "It does bring Zelda's to my mind. Only your ring's a warm and pleasing shade of green because the magic in it ain't fired by a cold and careless lust and greed."

"Gnat's ring's fired by the love in her heart." Miss Hope smiles at me and I see her gold tooth once again.

I love that tooth. It seems to hold out to me the promise of a new and exciting world. I'll need that world once Goodlow's reunited with Penelope.

"Gnat's ring has a healing power," Granny says.

"You think so?" I say. Eatmore Beans said the same thing.

"I know so," Granny says. "And I reckon now's the time for you to use that power to bring your momma into this mortal world where she can discover for herself love's mighty crystal.

"How do you think that you can do this, Gnat?" Granny stares hard at me.

"By helping Penelope to save Goodlow," I say.

"How can it be done?" Granny's eyes bear into mine. She's searching my heart. I still got that boy inside my heart. She says, "Goodlow can only be saved by a gal who truly loves him."

I still love him.

Why did Penelope have to break her arm? Things would be a whole lot easier if she hadn't broken that fool arm!

"I reckon I can stand in for Penelope," I finally say. "My arms can act for her arms. I reckon the power in my ring will help me." I can hope.

"If you can do it, Gnat, you'll save not only Goodlow, but also your momma and your own self," Granny says. "And I won't let you stand alone. I mean to have everyone in Mary's Cove there at the pond. They'll cheer you on and give you courage. For you are our Gnat."

"I'll stand beside you, Gnat." Penelope struggles to her feet. She puts her good arm around my waist and leans her head down with all its curly golden hair until it hits my shoulder and then, she rests it there. "I'll call out to Goodlow, 'Gnat's standing in for me. Trust our Gnat!' I'll shout encouragement all through your trials. And once you've thrown Goodlow into the pond and he comes back out, I'll have my green cloak ready to throw over him."

"That will save him for the long run." I bite my lip and then I say the hardest thing of all. "For it's you he belongs with, just like Eatmore Beans belongs with Baby Earl."

It's then that I take off the enchanted locket that's brought my heart to love. In front of Miss Hope with her sparkly tooth and Granny, I say to Penelope, "Good-low told me to give this to you," which is close to the truth. I put the necklace on over Penelope's head and now it hangs from her slender neck where I reckon it belongs.

Only once that locket's off, I . . . I still feel in love with Goodlow. I feel more in love with him than ever.

Is it because he kissed me?

He was the first boy to ever kiss me.

36

ranny Hart gets everyone so keyed up over the mission to save Goodlow, they force DeWitt Lawson to cancel my grandpa's trial! All but DeWitt agree that I can't be worried about my grandpa being put on trial; I need all my strength to take on Zelda. I tell everyone how my grandpa used the last drop of his moonshine to foil Zelda's Warrior Bogies so that I could follow a Swamp Cat to Goodlow. This causes Buffer McLeod, who's partial to moonshine himself, to shout into DeWitt's scowling face, "Nathaniel Stokes deserves a medal!"

He certainly does.

And now, it's drawing onto midnight and here we are—over a hundred of us, marching out through the still and ominous night air to the Hallelujah Pond. I'm grateful for everyone's support and company. But how all these folk will find room to hide themselves behind the changing sheds at the pond so that Zelda will not see them, I do not know. When I mentioned this to Granny, she just said, "We'll find a way."

I got my Darnell Army with me—even Baby Earl with Eatmore Beans. Baby Earl's warm hand holds on to mine. At my back, Wanda repeats for Baby Earl, Jib and me what Buffer McLeod told everyone moments earlier as we were about to leave the church—"We'll know Gnat's momma's on the march when we hear her wailing like a panther."

"Wailing like a panther," Jib repeats.

"After that, beneath our feet, we'll feel the galloping hoofbeats of Zelda's Swampers," Wanda says.

"Yup," Jib says. "We'll feel the galloping of them Swamp Knights on plow horses and the pale green ladies on the backs of giant salamanders. They'll come galloping, galloping, up and up through them dark caverns beneath Old Baldy Top Mountain, through Foggy Bottom, down Piney Gap Road and into Mary's Cove."

"We'll feel them hopping bogies," Wanda says.

"And the Boogety Bear—'Boogety, boogety,'" Jib says.

"You won't hear no Boogety Bear," I say.

"How come?" Jib sounds disappointed.

"He's done disappeared." I don't need to tell Jib that Goodlow's been the Boogety Bear all these years. She'd cast a suspicious eye on him to her dying day.

I'll love him until mine.

"There'll be Frank Gump and his crew," Jib says.

"I'll spit them skeletons in the eye," I say.

"You'll put out the fire in their eyes for good," Wanda says and I say, "Yes, Wanda, I will."

We march as stealthily as we can through eerie moonlight along with everyone else who's come in support of me and Penelope. All Hallows' Eve is here. Just ahead, Grandpa's talking about me to DeWitt Lawson and Buffer. My grandpa's saying, "I always knew my Gnat was someone special."

"That she is," Buffer says. "But is she a match for the Swamp Queen? That Queen's been around for hundreds of years."

"My Gnat's a match for anyone," Grandpa says.

Alongside them, Luther Pryce waves a Welcome Home Son hat he made in the air. The hat's covered in white polka dots so you can see it after dark. Will Goodlow get to see it? I hope.

A full moon shines. A harvest moon for All Hallows' Eve. It makes shadows of us all. I look down at Eatmore Beans. The cat, wide-eyed and perky looking, sits upright in Baby Earl's arms. I'd like the cat to talk to me— *Bad poem, lassie!* But the cat's with his own laddie now. I reckon I'll never hear Eatmore's words in my head ever again.

"It shouldn't be long before Eatmore Beans grows strong enough to walk on his own," I tell Baby Earl. "I hope after all is said and done, he don't change too much. I hope I'll still come upon him reading the newspapers on our cabin wall."

"Eatmore Beans don't like them newspapers," Baby Earl says. "He says they got too much talk of war and fighting in them."

"Well, you tell him Miss Hope has a whole passel of books for him to read instead—including one in particular, *Little Women*, which I'm sure he'll like." I hope DeWitt Lawson lets Miss Hope stay in Mary's Cove and be our teacher. I need me a teacher so bad, it hurts. She and her books can help me to get over Goodlow. Will they? There's always hope.

"I'll tell him all about them books, Gnat," Baby Earl says.

He whispers to Eatmore Beans while, ahead of us, Miss Hope helps Granny guide a green-cloaked Penelope with her long hair freshly brushed and shining golden in the moonlight around a tree. Studs Darnell stalks behind them. I'm sure he'd like to grab hold of Penelope and keep her for himself, but he can't because she still has on that dead toad. If all goes well, Penelope won't need to wear that toad no more.

She'll be with Goodlow.

Baby Earl shakes my hand.

"What is it, Baby Earl?" We're drawing close to the Hallelujah Pond. I can smell its water, made murky by all that swamp mud Zelda made Frank Gump and his Boys pour into it. Except, of course, for the middle.

"Eatmore Beans says when Zelda does that thing she does to Goodlow, you is not to look at her or else she will bewitch you," Baby Earl says.

"Well, don't you worry, Baby Earl." I lean down and whisper to him, "Do you know why?" He shakes his head. I whisper, "Because I'm bewitched already."

Bewitched by a kiss.

37

The Hallelujah Pond ain't all that big since Zelda's been messing with it. The pond's now about the size of Grandpa's bean patch. On the pond's northeast side, which lies open to the harvest moon (unlike the southwest side, gobbled up by prickly blackberry brambles), Preacher John's Lane crosses over Piney Gap Road. Piney Gap's a determined road. Starting in Gobbler's Glen, it crosses Old Baldy Top Mountain, shoots along the murky edge of Foggy Bottom, fords Tucker Creek, cuts through Mary's Cove, knifes its way through the southern mountains and eventually pierces the heart of Hell on Earth, Tennessee.

My momma and her Swampers should come parading out of Foggy Bottom, down Piney Gap and past the Hallelujah Pond at any moment. Ain't we already heard the Swamp Queen's panther scream? It sent us scrambling behind the changing stations on the pond's southwest side. Blackberry brambles have overtaken this side of the pond and I hadn't realized that until this very moment. Now we got over a hundred of us crowded inside them prickly brambles and it ain't comfortable.

The soles of our feet, scratched by prickers (all except for Jib—she's got on them shoes), still tremble from the rumbling of Zelda's Swampers, galloping, galloping up and up and out of the ground—*Zelda's coming. Zelda's coming.* The air smells like it does after lightning when you ain't had rain. Buffer, at the outside edge of the brambles, tugs on my arm and whispers, "They're here. They're here," while Penelope, hidden far deeper in the thorny brambles than I am because all of us just crowded in after her, is sobbing, "My hair. My hair."

"What's wrong with Penelope's hair?" I hiss at those behind me while the first group of Zelda's Swampers comes hopping around the nearby moonlit bend—hundreds of Warrior Bogies. They wave their stinging tentacles on high. They're followed by Zelda's crew—them skeletons—fire blazing from their dark eye sockets. Zelda's got their bones lit up so you can see them plain as day.

They don't scare me.

"Penelope's hair's caught up in prickers," I hear Miss Hope whisper to Granny, who whispers it to Wanda, who passes it on to Jib, who passes it on to Luther Pryce, who bellows it in Baby Earl's ear and then, Baby Earl, clutching my hand tight, passes it on to me.

"Tell her to get it unstuck real fast," I say.

The second group of Zelda's Swampers now comes trotting around the bend—a hoard of pale green ladies in long tattered dresses the color of rotted leaves and spotted with black mold. They ride on the backs of giant salamanders. Behind them, lather dripping from its mouth, pants a yellow Swamp Dog, followed by a pack of stinkpot turtles each ridden by a little polka-dotted Swamp Faerie.

Wish I could catch me one of them.

And now Zelda herself rounds the bend. My wicked, wicked momma. She rides bareback on a black plow horse at least eighteen hands high. He's a prancing stallion with pale blue eyes. He's got nervous sweat whitening his flanks.

Now, I've seen Zelda when she was a panther. And I've come upon her as a Voice. But I ain't never seen her as the Swamp Queen with her green ring burning cold and heartless in the moonlight. She's got cream white skin and wild curly auburn hair—like mine. She's long limbed and sharp featured like me and she's got on a purple dress, patched with yellow star-shaped sweet gum leaves. The dress fringe has got silver bells attached to it, which jingle with each prancing step her plow horse takes.

My momma looks coldhearted but pretty. I reckon if she was a thirty-seven-year-old mortal woman turning gray, she'd still look pretty. She don't see me standing at the edge of the blackberry patch—studying her real close-like while I finger the ring she put in my baby basket.

Granny, who's worked her way past the brambles to me, whispers in my ear, "Gnat, you're a brave gal with a heart made strong by love and you got on a magic ring—more powerful than your momma's. I know that with it, you will do what's right."

"Yes, Granny, I will." I do have me a heart of love. I do have me that ring.

"You got all of Mary's Cove to back you," Granny says as ten Swamp Knights on hoary old plow horses round the bend. Behind them knights, with their long swords drawn and their pop-out eyes looking this way and that, rides Goodlow on his pure white mule. He looks handsomer than ever. He's a prince in black shirt and trousers with a bearskin cape falling from his shoulders.

My poor heart leaps as soon as I see him.

38

Somewhere deep in the prickers behind me, Penelope is calling out: "Hold on, Gnat. Wait for me. I'm coming." But she's not coming fast enough. Goodlow's passing the Hallelujah Pond right now! His left hand dangles down, waiting for a gal who truly loves him to grab it. I can't wait for Penelope!

Hissing to Granny, "Tell Penelope to get out here fast," I step forth from the blackberry patch. Not looking at anyone but Goodlow, I run up to his white mule and grab it by the bridle. The mule stops dead.

Goodlow stares down at me, dumbfounded.

"Daughter!" my momma shrieks. I don't look at her, but I can tell by the jingling of her bells, she's turning her black plow horse to face me. "You don't belong here!"

"Ma Stokes!" I name her for what she is. "I do!"

"*Ma Stokes?*" she screams.

I go to grab Goodlow's dangling hand. He lifts it away from me. He ain't gonna let me grab his hand! He don't trust me. He thinks I betrayed him. I yell at him,

"I brought your sweetheart here. She's coming to you. Only I'm standing in for her because she broke her arm and then got stuck in them blackberry bushes."

He glances at them bushes and suddenly, he don't look dumbfounded no more, for now his sweetheart bravely limps forth from them, carrying her green cloak over her one good arm, and she's got more pricker scratches on her than a dog has fleas. The rest of Mary's Cove files out behind her.

It hurts to see the loving way Goodlow looks at Penelope. My momma chuckles. In a voice colder than well water she says to Goodlow, "Your sweetheart's done broke her arm. You ain't got no one to save you from the devil now."

"Yes he does!" I scream at her.

To Goodlow, I say, "There is someone who can save you. That someone is me. Take my hand. Soon as you do, my hand becomes Penelope's. My heart becomes hers. And if this ain't true love on my part for you, I don't know what is."

He holds out his hand to me.

Finally, at last, I grab his hand and I pull him off his mule.

My momma screams as if she's being torn in two. She turns Goodlow into a raging bull! Instead of a boy, I got me the long curved horns of an angry black bull in my two hands. The bull dips his nose under me. He tosses me so high into the air, I ain't got no ground beneath my feet. He shakes me like I was a rag doll. I hear Penelope shouting, "Hold him, Gnat," as he flings me up and down and sideways.

I hold on.

"Zip-Zap, turtle snap!" Zelda shrieks and she turns Goodlow into a giant snapping turtle. I got me a giant snapping turtle in my hands. That turtle tries to bite my nose. I duck to one side then the other. Penelope shouts, "Keep ducking, Gnat." Folks join in, "Duck, Gnat, duck!" I duck. I hold on. I don't let the precious Goodlow go.

"Pizzat to that!" my momma shrieks and now, instead of a snapping turtle, I got me a snarling panther by the tail. Holding on, I lean backward and I spin real fast in circles with that panther so it can't whirl around and slash at me with its fangs and claws.

"Hang on, Gnat!" Penelope screams.

"Hang on!" folks scream.

I hang on. I become real dizzy and my hands grow tired, but I don't let the panther go.

And suddenly, I ain't holding on to that panther no more, but a bar of molten iron. Zelda has turned Goodlow Pryce into a bar of hot iron burning up my hands. I tell myself, "This don't hurt me none because I got on a magic ring."

"Gnat, look at me," Zelda shrieks.

Now, Eatmore Beans has warned me not to look at the Swamp Queen when she does her thing because she'll bewitch me. But I'm already bewitched by Goodlow. I give the Swamp Queen a quick glance sideways. She raises her right hand, which has on its fourth finger a ring like mine. And she shouts at me, "Let that fool boy go! If you don't let him go, I'll lose him and you besides! He'll burn you to a crisp."

Well, I ain't listening to her! I hold tight to my Goodlow. He sets me on fire. My hands. My arms. My dress. My hair. They all catch fire. I am a fiery conflagration. Folks are shouting at me, but I'm burning so hot and fierce, I can't hear a word they say.

And then, within the roaring of the flames, I hear a voice I thought I'd never hear again. It's Eatmore Beans—word-thoughting me:

Lassie, if you truly love him, let him go.

And so I do.

Screaming, "I love you, Goodlow!" I throw what's left of him into the deep center of the Hallelujah Pond. And then, because I am on fire, I throw myself into the pond as well. As I sink down into the calm and soothing pond water, I hear my momma wail, "I'm mortal. I'm mortal!"

That momma sure ain't no Swedish Nightingale.

39

The next thing I know, I'm being hauled from the water and up onto the bank by Wanda and Jib with Baby Earl and Eatmore Beans looking down on me real worried-like and Grandpa Stokes shouting, "Gnat, you ain't got no clothes on!"

I look down. Glory be. The fire's done burned up my new dress, but it looks like I am still here in my entirety.

"Don't you worry, Gnat, my cloak's big enough to cover you and Goodlow, both," Penelope says. She orders them Darnells to lay me next to Goodlow, who ain't a bar of iron no more but a naked real-life boy. His skin looks as bright and clean as mine does.

Penelope tucks her soft green cloak around us both and he smiles up at her.

He loves her.

"You're our hero, Gnat," Wanda whispers in my right ear. Jib, crowding next to her, says, "Soon as you threw Goodlow and yourself into the pond, all them Swampers including Zelda disappeared into a poof of smoke, even them turtles, giant salamanders and horses they was riding. Zelda kept complaining, 'I'm mortal. I'm mortal.'"

Now, what am I going to do with a mortal thirty-seven-year-old mother? I'm sure I'll think of something only right now I'm plumb wore out. I'm so wore out, I want to sleep. And so I do. I sleep for three days. When I finally wake up, I discover something remarkable about myself. Instead of having one brown and one green eye, I now got me two green ones. Them Darnells say it happened when I threw myself into the Hallelujah Pond. The water caused my magic ring to melt, turning the whole pond green and my brown eye, too.

With my two green eyes has come the second sight like Granny has. With the second sight I can see things hidden, far away and into the future. You won't believe what I saw. In one of those glimpses, I saw my pappy strolling down Piney Gap in this direction. Spring green leaves were on the trees. He had his fiddle tucked under one arm and my momma hanging on to the other. Them two were carrying on! I ain't sure what they were fighting about, but I could tell from the fierce tears in my momma's eyes that she was upset with Pappy, which means she cares for him. My momma now has a heart! There ain't nothing like a heart. You ain't alive without one.

I'll reckon I'll have a lot to talk over with them two when they get here.

A whole passel of folk followed after them—including Preacher John. Everyone wants to come to Mary's Cove on account of our Hallelujah Pond—now known as the Miracle Pond. DeWitt Lawson named it. I'll tell you why.

The day after my ring had turned the pond green, Miss Hope and DeWitt went out walking by it and them two had an argument about having a school in Mary's Cove. Miss Hope said we needed one. DeWitt, still upset about the cancellation of my grandpa's trial and feeling ornery because of it, said, "We ain't got time nor money to build a school!" Them two carried on, the upshot being Miss Hope pushed DeWitt Lawson in the pond! The water cured him of his dander, which is a real miracle! He's been a changed man ever since.

I knew Miss Hope was someone special.

Now DeWitt's helping Buffer, Grandpa Stokes and others to build us a school. Meanwhile, Miss Hope has started classes in Granny's cabin. I sit in the front row along with Jib, Wanda, Baby Earl and Eatmore Beans. Along with English grammar, mathematics, Latin, history and poetry, we're studying how to put the war behind us so that we can live in peace with our Rebel kin and others. For my part, I've ripped all the Union-minded and incendiary war articles off our cabin walls and I'm replacing them with sheets of love poetry Miss Hope's helping me to write.

Life's improving in Mary's Cove. We even got us back our rainbow. Starting at the pond, that rainbow ends wherever Penelope and Goodlow can be found together.

I let Goodlow go.

Granny says letting go's the hardest side of love and I'll admit I still got problems with it. What helps is that, for bedtime reading, Miss Hope has lent me *Little Women*. Each night, I read *Little Women* aloud to them Darnells and Eatmore Beans.

Now in *Little Women*, there's a boy called Laurie. He ain't got no momma to speak of and he lives with his grandpa—same as me. Laurie's in love with a gal named Jo. But Laurie ain't the right boy for her in the long run and it's sad when he finds that out.

Here's my favorite part. I've read it to myself a hundred times and now you can read it, too:

"Laurie thought that the task of forgetting his love for Jo would absorb all his powers for years; but, to his great surprise, he discovered it grew easier every day. He refused to believe it at first, got angry with himself, and couldn't understand it; but these hearts of ours are curious and contrary things, and time and nature work their will in spite of us."

Time and nature work their will in spite of us.

I reckon they both can and do.

Acknowledgements

I owe a debt of gratitude to my editor, Patricia Lee Gauch, who, when I told her how much I loved the Scottish ballad, Tam Lin, suggested I retell the story and set it in the Appalachian Mountains. I am also deeply indebted to Louisa May Alcott, author of Little Women—a remarkable book that for well over a century has touched the hearts of many including a certain gal living high in an isolated mountain cove, Gnat Stokes.